Knight Moves
Black Knight Chronicles, Vol.3

For Laura~
Thanks + Enjoy!

Con Carolinas
2012

Knight Moves

Black Knight Chronicles, Vol. 3

By John G. Hartness

Falstaff Books
Charlotte, NC

For information on appearances, signings, autographed
copies, etc. please visit
http://www.johnhartness.com
@johnhartness on Twitter

Knight Moves is dedicated to Suzy,
my continual source of inspiration

Also by John G. Hartness

Chapter 1

I woke up with a beautiful woman staring down at me, her brown curls cascading over my face. I smiled into the dark eyes of Detective Sabrina Law. "This is a nice way to start an evening. I love the way your hair smells." She straddled my waist fully dressed, but I had faith in my ability to fix that. Then I noticed she wasn't returning my smile. Her expression wavered between betrayed and furious, and her green eyes were red-rimmed. I smelled the salt on her cheek and raised my head a little, surprised when she pulled back, scowling.

"Don't move," she said in a low, tense voice.

Not being one to listen much, I tried to sit up, then realized I was handcuffed to my bed. While not my normal thing, I wasn't going to ask questions until I realized that the handcuffs were silver-plated, and that my skin was starting to blister from the exposure. I pulled experimentally at the restraints, got nowhere, then tried to move my legs with a similar lack of results. I started to get a little worried. When I saw that Sabrina still hadn't so much as cracked a smile, I *really* started to worry. When I noticed the silver stake she had pressed against my chest, I became downright concerned.

"I didn't mean it. Those jeans definitely do not make your butt look big." I smiled, giving my best disarming look, to no avail. No surprise there. I'd always been the guilty-looking one, even before I became an undead creature of the night.

Sabrina looked down, disgust and anger coming off of her in waves, and poked the stake a little harder into my chest. "Give me one good reason why I shouldn't shove this overgrown toothpick into your heart right now."

"Ummm... my sparkling personality?" I tried one more time for humor, but my jokes were falling flatter than usual.

"Not even close, you parasite." She pulled her arm back as if to jam the stake home, but just before she perforated me, she very quietly asked, "How could you?"

"How could I what?" I asked, just as quietly. I figured if a little quiet time was what the situation demanded, I shouldn't argue. Besides, I had no idea why she was angry. I was no stranger to inspiring violence in other people, especially women, but this time I couldn't come up with anything I had done to her specifically. And since it was close to impossible for me to get blackout drunk anymore, my memory was pretty solid.

"You know what, you monster!" She poked the stake into my

chest a little. I couldn't see what was going on, but I heard a sizzling sound as the silver came into contact with my blood.

I hadn't known my blood would boil when touched by silver. "No, really, I don't have any idea what you're talking about! And you know my "stupid face" by now!" I tried again to twist away from the pointy bit.

"You murdered a girl tonight, Jimmy. You drained her dry and left her in a construction site. I saw the body, and I know a vampire kill when I see one. She was just a kid, and you threw her aside like a piece of garbage. I thought I knew you. How could you do that?" The look of betrayal in her eyes hurt almost as much as the silver stake. Almost, but not quite. Really, not even close to as much, but it still hurt.

"Sabrina, what the hell are you talking about? You know me better than that! I could never do that to someone." I pulled against my restraints, desperate to do something, anything to make her stop looking at me as though I were a monster.

"I don't know anything about you." She just kept looking at me, eyes full of betrayal. That part hurt the worst, the look.

I twisted around again, then looked her in the eyes. "Sabrina, I swear to you, I didn't kill anyone tonight. I didn't even eat takeout! I was here all night with Greg watching *Being Human* reruns on Netflix. Go ask the svelte avenger if you don't believe me!"

"No need to go anywhere, Detective. He's telling the truth. And please get off of my partner. You're distraught, and I'd hate for you to make a mistake and let him live." Greg Knightwood, my partner and roommate, stood in the doorway to my bedroom wearing, of all things, baby-blue footie pajamas. A forty-year-old vampire in footie pajamas. I wasn't sure which was worse, that I had to be rescued by the fat half of our Laurel and Hardy duo, or that he did it wearing footie pajamas. I finally decided that the pj-wearing was the worst part.

"Besides, I think he's starting to enjoy it a little too much," Greg added.

Sabrina blushed and got off of me, but she didn't remove the cuffs. "Why should I believe you, Greg?" She got right up in my partner's face. To be precise about it, she got way over my partner's head because she had a couple inches on him, especially in her ass-kicking, dark red leather boots. I guessed when you were going to kill your friend, you dressed for the occasion.

"Because I didn't shoot you in the back of the head." Greg raised his 9mm, then holstered the weapon. I wasn't sure where he kept a holster in his jammies, but right then I wasn't interested in asking a whole lot of questions. "Now, shall we have a drink and talk about this like civilized people?" He turned and walked toward the living room. Sabrina watched his retreating back for a moment, looked back at me, then followed him.

"Hey kids, not for nothing, but you wanna uncuff me first? I gotta pee."

*****

A few minutes later, we were all settled in the living room. I had taken a few minutes to attend to nature's call and pull on some sweats and a t-shirt, while Greg had gotten three beers out of the fridge. I grabbed one and sat next to Greg on the sofa, with Sabrina in the armchair comfortably out of staking range.

I took a long pull off my beer and tried to figure out where I'd gone wrong. Last time I checked, Sabrina and I were moving, admittedly at a glacial pace, from "bickering acquaintances" to "something undefined that might have potential to be very interesting if there were enough liquor in the house on a Saturday night." Now I had to re-evaluate all that, given the burns on my wrist and the little bloody spots her stake had left in my chest. Just my luck, the one cute girl I met since I died and, six months later, she wanted to kill me. Again.

I propped my feet on the coffee table. "Now, would you like to tell me exactly what had you so riled up you wanted to puncture my internal organs?"

Sabrina had the good grace to look a little embarrassed. "Tonight, about two o'clock, I caught a call. Young white female found dead at a construction site near the university. I rolled out there to take a look, and the cause of death made you the prime suspect. Sorry about that." She glanced down at the stake in her hands, blushed, and tucked it away in a jacket pocket.

"What was the cause of death?" I asked around a mouthful of Miller Lite.

"Exsanguination."

"What's that?"

"She was drained of blood, moron," Greg chimed in.

"Why does not knowing what exsanguination means make me a moron?"

"Because exsanguination is kinda our thing, doofus. You should at least recognize the term."

"Good point. I hate the fact that my partner is the smart one. Why did I have to be burdened with stunning good looks?" I asked

12

the ceiling of our basement apartment. It didn't answer, and I supposed I would have been a bit concerned if it had.

"Anyway," Sabrina tried to get us back on track, "when I examined the body, I saw that not only had she been drained of all blood, the only wounds I found were two holes in the side of her neck."

"So you immediately jumped to the completely unfounded conclusion that I was responsible? Thanks a lot. I thought you knew me better than that."

"Well, Greg never bites people, and you two are the only vampires in town." She wouldn't look at me and, right at that moment, I didn't mind. I was more than a little crazy about the sexy police detective, but it stung a lot more than my pride that she thought I was a murderer.

"So the logical conclusion is that you're the killer, Jimmy. Now, when were you going to teach me that trick of being in two places at once?" My partner smirked a little at Sabrina's embarrassment and my sulking.

"Why?" I shot back. "So you can be at Lazer Tag and the comic book store at the same time?" Not my best effort, but I was still upset. I hadn't woken up to many good-looking women lately, and this one had threatened my life. I was more than somewhat distressed.

"So, now what? Since Jimmy obviously isn't the killer, where do you look next?" Greg asked Sabrina.

"I have no idea. The crime lab guys are going over the scene for trace evidence, but it's a construction site. That's going to make narrowing down the evidence tough."

"Yeah," Greg agreed. "With so many people coming and going, there's no way to tell who left a particular print."

"No way for the *police* to tell," I said, getting up and heading toward my bedroom without further explanation.

"Huh?" Sabrina asked. "What are you talking about?"

"We have a few advantages that your crime scene techs don't have," Greg explained. He obviously got where I was going with this, since he got up and headed for his bedroom.

"Where are you two going?" Sabrina yelled from the den.

"To get dressed. You don't think I'm going anywhere near a bunch of armed men while he's wearing his Transformers PJs, do you?"

"They're not Transformers!" Greg yelled from his bedroom. They really were. I was pretty sure that was a vintage Optimus Prime right in the center of his chest.

Chapter 2

"Yup, it's a construction site, all right."

Greg and I got out of my car at the big hole in the ground where the university was building its latest monument to knowledge—a football stadium.

"What was your first clue, Sherlock?" Sabrina asked, as she walked up behind me.

"Not sure if it was the heavy machinery or the big signs that said 'Construction - Keep Out.'" She started a little at my gruff tone, but I hadn't quite forgiven her yet. I walked ahead of her until I met a serious-looking young cop who seemed a little green around the gills. "Rough night?" I asked, as I got to the crime scene tape he was guarding.

"Yeah, it's a bad one." That proved he hadn't seen very many dead people. For one thing, vampire kills weren't usually that unattractive. We didn't like to waste food, so there wasn't much blood splatter. Since there wasn't as much blood in a smaller body, we typically didn't go after children, either. So most of the things that made veteran cops call a crime scene a "bad one" weren't normally present.

So I figured the kid would be easy. I ducked under the crime scene tape and started to push past him, muttering, "I heard it wasn't pretty," but for all the fresh puke on his uniform shoes, the kid wasn't going to let his job slide. He put a hand on my chest and stopped me, mostly because I let him.

"I need to see your ID, Detective," he said, deferentially. I glared, and he ducked his head. "Sorry, but those are my orders, and I don't know everybody yet."

"Don't worry, Jenkins. If you did know him, you really would have had reason to stop him," Sabrina's voice came from behind me. "But he's with me, so it's okay."

I actually heard the kid's heart rate speed up when Sabrina came into view. It would have been cute if I hadn't still been annoyed with her. "Yes, sir. I mean, ma'am. I mean…"

"It's okay kid, she gets that 'sir' bit a lot." I pushed past the stammering patrolman and headed into the site where they were pouring the foundation of the stadium. The crime scene techs were crawling all over the place, but I gave them a little *ignore-me* mojo, and walked straight over to the body.

14

The kid had been right. This was a bad one, not because it was gruesome, but because it was actually a little bit beautiful, in a macabre sort of way. The victim was a blond-haired girl, maybe twenty years old. It was hard for me to judge height with her lying down, but she was very petite, maybe five-foot-one and a hundred pounds soaking wet. She'd been drained; I could tell from the look of her flesh. And the smell. Dead people had a very distinct smell because blood went bad very quickly. Almost immediately after the owner died, blood began to sour, until just a few hours later it became poisonous to beings like me. A sip could cause violent convulsions, and drinking too much from a corpse would kill all but the strongest vampire. You do not want to know how I came by that very painful bit of knowledge.

But this girl had none of that bad-blood smell, and there wasn't a drop of blood on the ground around her. From a distance, she almost appeared to be asleep. Very, very pale, but asleep. Except that she lay perfectly still, without even the slightest breath or twitch of an eyelid. She was posed in a prone position on a section of finished concrete slab, blue eyes staring into nothing, just beginning to film over in death. Her hands were intertwined behind her head, and one leg was cocked to the side in a distinctive "come hither" posture. It was like she was trying to be sexy, but ended up dead instead. She wore jeans and a gold and green university sweatshirt, with the pickaxe 49ers logo emblazoned across her childlike chest. A pair of sensible sneakers completed the look, but something seemed off somehow. I stood there, taking in the whole scene, until it came to me.

"Where's her backpack?" I asked Sabrina.

Her head came up, and she locked eyes with me, startled. "What backpack?"

"She was obviously coming from class, so where's her backpack?"

"And how was she *obviously* coming from class?" a new voice asked. I glanced over Sabrina's shoulder to see Lieutenant Joseph McDaniel glowering at me and Greg as if we were something he'd scraped off his shoe. He was wrong; we were nowhere near classy enough to hang around his shoes. The lieutenant was a well-dressed black man in a neatly pressed suit and wore shoes that cost more than my entire wardrobe—not Greg's because, unfortunately, spandex was expensive. It wasn't really unfortunate that spandex was expensive, it was just unfortunate that Greg owned spandex. Lt. McDaniel was Sabrina's boss and, in the past, he had made it very clear that her association with us was bad for her career.

15

I tried for about half a second to keep my mouth from going into overdrive, but it was never going to work. I'd woken up with a beautiful woman on top of me for all the wrong reasons and was now looking at a very pretty waste of a life in the middle of a pile of concrete dust and red mud, so my natural snark boiled right to surface. "Well, Lieutenant, I'm guessing that your M.E. will tell you time of death was sometime around ten p.m. That's about the time the last evening class ends on a weeknight and, since this girl isn't dressed for clubbing, she was either coming from the library, the student union, or a class. And since the library is on the other side of campus, the student center is nowhere close to here, and there aren't any residence halls nearby, it makes the most sense that she was taking the most direct route from that class building," I gestured to an imposing brick building behind us, "to those apartments." I pointed to a set of rundown campus apartments just visible through some trees. I could see a well-worn path through the sparse woods, but I was blessed with better vision than most people. Of course, I had to die to get my super-vision, so the jury was still out on whether or not it had been a fair trade.

Lieutenant McDaniel looked like he'd bitten into something sour but, after a few seconds, he grudgingly admitted, "That's about what we figured, too. So who or what do you *special consultants* think did this?" I looked over at Greg for help. Unsure what McDaniel was playing at by calling us "consultants," I didn't want to stick my foot in my mouth if there was the chance for a raise on the line. Since most of our work for the police department had been *pro bono* to this point, anything would be a raise.

Greg had fortunately decided that discretion was the better part of valor and had left his utility belt and spandex costume at home. He almost looked like a normal person in a pair of black cargo pants and a black sweater. I knew what kinds of toys he had stashed in the pockets of those pants but, if he was going to bail me out with McDaniel, I figured I wouldn't blow his cover. He raised his hand, and said, "If I may?" McDaniel nodded.

"At this point we have no idea how she was subdued but, even from here, we can see that the young lady was obviously exsanguinated. Your cause of death will be extreme blood loss, but the methodology of said exsanguination is what is in question. Obviously, her left carotid artery was punctured with some type of needle, and the blood drained and removed from the scene. It appears from a rudimentary examination that the murderer made two holes in the neck, either to speed the blood flow, or for some other reason."

16

"Maybe he missed on the first try?" I suggested. Anything to deflect from the truth—the girl had been bitten by a vampire and drained completely of blood. I knew that both fangs had gone into the artery, because vampires didn't miss, at least not after the first couple of meals. And by the way he had posed the victim after he finished, I knew the guy had been killing people for a long time.

"He didn't miss. Both punctures went into the carotid artery, and she would have bled out in minutes. Now, if you'll excuse me." I looked around for the new voice and saw Bobby Reed wheeling a stretcher over to the body. We were drawing a crowd, about the last thing I wanted in the predawn hours. We needed to wrap this up pretty quickly, or Greg and I were going to have some serious radiation poisoning.

Bobby was the coroner's assistant and our main blood supplier at the county hospital, so he was nowhere on the list of people I wanted to see at a crime scene where a vampire was the obvious killer. He didn't say a word to us, or do anything to indicate he knew us from Adam's housecat; he just started bagging up the body and wheeling it to the ambulance. When I saw Bobby load the stretcher into the back of the ambulance, I was suddenly hit with a very unpleasant realization.

I looked over at Greg and saw his eyes widen, too. We'd both realized the same thing at the same time; the corpse had been completely drained. And all indications pointed to a vampire doing the draining. That meant that if we didn't do something, and quickly, that little coed was going to wake up soon with an aversion to sunlight and a new set of dietary restrictions. And she was going to wake up *hungry*.

Chapter 3

When Bobby had the body loaded and rolled off, I grabbed Sabrina and made a pretense of looking over the trail back to the classroom building. Once we were out of earshot of the other humans at the crime scene, I leaned toward her, and said "We've gotta get to the hospital. Now."

"Why, what's wrong?"

"That little girl was drained. We gotta go."

"I know she was drained. That's why she's dead, Jimmy."

"Yeah, dead for now. And if you want her to stay that way, we're gonna have to cut off her head."

"What are you babbling about? She's dead. People who are dead tend to stay that way in my experience. And I'm a homicide detective, which gives me an unwelcome degree of familiarity with dead people."

"Hi. Jimmy Black, walking dead man. Have we met? Sabrina, that little girl was drained *completely*. By a *vampire*. If my math is right, that means we've got about, oh… no time to get to the body before she wakes up a as brand new little vampire hottie. A very, very hungry vampire hottie. And since Bobby has a certain amount of usefulness to me, I'd rather he not end up as her first entree. So, can you get me there?"

Sabrina turned almost as pale when my words sank in. She looked around to make sure no one had overheard. "No problem, but what about Greg?"

"He's going to stay here to investigate and keep Lieutenant McSmartypants occupied. Now, let's move. We've got an ambulance to hijack." Without saying a word to anyone else, we walked quickly to Sabrina's car and headed after Bobby and his lethal cargo.

"By the way," I said, as Sabrina pulled onto the main road heading into town. "Where did you get a silver stake?" No way was I letting her live that down.

"I ordered it online after we first met. I meant to throw it away when I realized you were one of the good guys, but…"

"But you never got around to it?"

"Yeah, something like that."

"Am I?" I watched my reflection in the window as the city rolled past us in the early morning gloom.

"Are you what?"

"Am I one of the good guys?"

She took a long time to answer, but finally whispered, "Yes." I looked over at her, but she wouldn't face me. I decided that was all the apology I was likely to get, so I let it go. If there was anything between us, we'd have to see if it survived the night.

I watched her speed through red lights for a few seconds. "You should probably keep it close by. At least for the next few nights."

She glanced over at me, surprised. "Why?"

"I didn't drink that girl, and Greg didn't drink that girl. But somebody did. And with whoever that somebody is, your gun isn't going to be much use."

"Oh." We were saved from saying anything more by the lights of the ambulance coming into view ahead.

"How do you want to do this?" I asked, as we pulled up tight behind the emergency vehicle. As with the norm for dead passengers, Bobby ran lights, but no siren, and obeyed the speed limit. After all, his cargo wasn't in any hurry for anything. At least as far as he knew.

"I thought I'd pull them over, and you'd mojo him into oblivion, then we'd figure out what to do about the girl." I already knew what we had to do about the girl, but Sabrina obviously wasn't quite ready to talk openly about it.

"Well, it sounds like as much of a plan as we ever have. Let's do this."

She nodded and pulled around the ambulance, blue lights flashing from behind her sun visors. She waved the ambulance driver over to the side of the road, and we both got out.

Bobby rolled down his window but didn't get out. "What's going on?"

"Turn off the vehicle; we need to talk to you," Sabrina yelled over the blaring siren. Bobby complied and joined us behind Sabrina's car.

"Oh," he said, as he caught sight of me. "It's you." His tone was flat, a little angry.

"What's with the attitude, Bobby?" I asked.

"I saw what happened to that girl. I know what you are. And I'm not stupid. I put two and two together, and I got you killing this chick. And that ain't right, man." I tried to interrupt, but he was obviously on a roll. Bobby went right on talking over me, and that doesn't happen often. "Regardless of our business arrangement, and the fact that I might feel a little betrayed to think you're dissing the service I provide and taking your meals on the hoof these days, I don't hold with killing. Especially not with killing *cute* chicks!"

Sabrina arched an eyebrow. "But it's okay to kill ugly girls?"

"There's a surplus of ugly in the world, Detective, but a finite number of hotties. It doesn't do to be taking them out of circulation."

I jumped in before things went from absurd to downright bloody. "Okay, Bobby, I get your point. But we've got two problems here. One, I didn't kill that girl. So get off your high horse. That means there's another vampire in town that none of us knew about before tonight."

"What's the second problem?" At my mention of another vampire, Bobby suddenly looked a lot less sure of himself.

"Your cargo was drained completely. That means she's going to wake up a vampire. A very hungry vampire. I don't think you want to be the first thing she lays eyes on when that happens."

"Oh, crap."

"*Oh, crap* is right. Now get in the car with Sabrina. And find some way to bloody your nose."

"Huh? Why?"

"Because I'm going to take care of this, and that means you need to get hijacked. This is just more guessing on my part, but I don't think you want me punching you in the face any more than you want to be Blood-Bank-Barbie's first meal." And of course, I heard it—the unmistakable sound of an industrial-strength zipper opening inside the ambulance.

"Bobby?"

"Yeah?"

"You want to be running now." I grabbed his arm and spun him toward Sabrina. She shot me a startled look, but I just growled, "Drive."

Sabrina and Bobby ran for her car just as the formerly pretty young coed kicked the ambulance's rear door open from the inside. What had been tragically beautiful when she lay dead at a construction site was just horrifying now. She dragged pieces of the body bag behind her as she came out of the ambulance, and her face showed nothing more than hunger and insanity. It had been a long time since I'd seen a newly awakened vampire and, while cuter than Greg at his coming-out party, she was no less raving. Her fangs were fully extended, and her eyes rolled in their sockets, as if they wouldn't focus. Then, suddenly, they did. She locked her eyes onto me like a pit bull on a sirloin, then leapt out of the ambulance.

If I'd still been alive, I would have died. Since I'd been dead a lot longer than she had, I was able to roll with her and throw her to the pavement. I glanced up to see Sabrina's taillights peeling back into traffic and caught a fist right on the chin for my trouble.

"Ow!" I yelled. "Cut that out!" The newly dead vamp didn't answer, just jumped at me again, jaws snapping on air as I spun out of her path. I had a flashback to Greg's first morning as a vampire, and that didn't help me focus on the fight. Not to mention, the chick was super-fast. Like faster than me fast, and I was no slouch in the speed department. She must have been in really good shape when she was alive or something.

Fortunately for me, she was completely, animal-growling, bite-the-dirt insane, or I would have been toast. Since she couldn't focus on anything for more than a couple of seconds, I was able to come up with a plan that seemed only somewhat ridiculous. The next time she lunged, I grabbed her arm and flung her back into the ambulance. As she crashed into the meat wagon, I reached to the side to slam the door shut on her.

Except… she bent the door beyond repair when she kicked it open again. I still held the half-closed door when the new vampire launched herself out of the back of the ambulance once more, taking me down and latching her teeth onto my shoulder. Between banging my head on the asphalt and getting holes in my favorite Spider Jerusalem t-shirt, it was not shaping up to be a very good night. I grabbed her by the hair and tried to pull her off me, but she was stuck tighter than a tick in July. I lurched to my feet, but she just wrapped her legs around my middle and kept drinking. *Is this what the folks felt like in Alien when the face-huggers got them?* I thought, as I felt my strength start to fade. The more she drank, the stronger she got. The stronger she got, the weaker I got. I was really starting to hate the merry-go-round.

I knew I had to do something fast, so I rammed her into the back bumper of the ambulance with all my strength. I heard ribs crack, and she opened her mouth to scream. The second her teeth pulled out of my flesh, I shoved one arm under her chin, keeping those teeth at bay, while I punched her in the side of the head with my other fist. After three or four solid shots to the temple, her legs relaxed from around my waist, and she slumped to the ground. I sagged down to sit on the bumper and drew my Glock, leveling it at her forehead.

The Glock was loaded with hollow points, so I was pretty sure I could decapitate her, or at least do enough damage to keep her dead, but something made me stop before I pulled the trigger. I thought back to Greg on his first night as a vampire, how out of control he had been. This kid was just like that, probably just like I had been when I attacked my best friend and accidentally turned him. My finger tightened on the trigger again, but I couldn't do it. It wasn't my fault she had been turned, but it wasn't my place to kill her, either. As of this moment, she was innocent. She hadn't hurt anyone, at least not anyone alive, and she didn't deserve to die because of what had been done to her. If I ever found out who turned her, that would be a different story. I put the Glock back in my shoulder holster and reached out to touch her shoulder.

She shook her head and growled as her eyes came into focus. "Who the hell are you?" she asked, wiping my blood off her lips with the back of one hand. "And where am I?"

"I think you're going to have a lot more questions in about an hour but, for now, let me give you the basics. My name is Jimmy. You're on the side of North Tryon Street at about six in the morning. You've been turned into a vampire. I'm one, too, and we have about half an hour to get inside before we both end up like my last attempt at a Thanksgiving turkey. And trust me, that wasn't pretty."

"Are you high or something?"

"Or something. For now, like they say in the movies, 'come with me if you want to live.'" I limped around to the front of the ambulance, got in, and started the engine. The girl sat on the pavement looking confused. And bloody. And cute. Which made for a terrible combination, especially since it was *my* blood. "You coming? Or dying?"

"Why should I believe you? What if you're a nut-job serial killer?" She reached into her pocket, where she probably carried pepper spray. Before the world and a hungry vamp made sure she'd never need pepper spray again.

"I haven't killed you yet, have I? And I'm the one with the gun. If I wanted you dead, you'd be dead." A little stretch on my part, because she was already dead, and I hadn't wanted it. I hadn't really wanted her to wake up, either. But I couldn't change that, so I had to be responsible for her. Greg was going to *love* this. He'd wanted a puppy for years, and I kept saying no, then I go and bring home a pet vampire.

She stared at me distrustfully. I looked at the brightening horizon, and said, "Look, Pumpkin, time's a-wasting. You can either come with me and maybe die, or stay here and definitely die. But I'm leaving. Now." She stared at me for a second or two longer, then got up in a ridiculously fluid motion and was at the passenger door in less time than it took me to blink twice. She got in and buckled up, and I headed off into the sunrise, trying the whole way to figure out where I was going to park an ambulance in our cemetery. Yeah, Greg was gonna love this.

Chapter 4

"You did what?" Greg stood gaping in the middle of our den, a forgotten game of *Left 4 Dead 2* on the big screen behind him.

"Are you insane?" Sabrina agreed from where she stood, back to a wall and service pistol pointed at the girl's head.

"What was I supposed to do?" I shielded the girl from Sabrina's aim with my body. I was at least forty-five percent sure she wouldn't shoot me, quite an improvement from earlier in the evening. "She bit me and drank enough to become aware. I couldn't kill her then."

"Wait a minute!" The girl stepped out from behind me. "You were going to kill me? And now you say you were rescuing me? What the hell? I'm out of here." She turned on her heel and headed toward the stairs, only to run into my oldest living friend Mike Maloney, who was on the way down to our apartment. Yeah, we kind of live underground. It helps with the whole encroaching sunlight problem we would run into with a penthouse. Plus, it was a lot cheaper.

"James, why is there an ambulance under a blue tarp in your front yard? And where might you be going, my child?" Mike put out an arm to stop her, but she brushed past him with ease. A little too much ease, in fact, since Mike went flying across the room. I intercepted him before he crashed into anything structural and put him down gently.

"Sorry, Dad. She doesn't know her own strength yet," I said.

"Obviously." Mike's hands shook as he made his way to the armchair and sat down heavily. He looked thin, and he smelled funny. Not funny ha-ha, but bad funny. Humans wouldn't be able to smell it, but it was obvious to me. I filed it away to ask him about later and turned my attention to the crisis at hand.

The girl had made it to the top of the stairs, and I heard the front door open, then slam shut an instant later. Just as quick, it opened again, and she dashed back down the stairs, smoke pouring from her clothes, and her skin flaking like the worst sunburn you've ever heard of. Greg and I shared a look and both shrugged. I headed to the fridge. I reached into the crisper, got four of our last five bags of blood and a couple of beers, then walked over to where the girl paced and cursed around at the bottom of the stairs.

I handed her a bag of blood. "Drink this."

"You have got to be kidding me." She threw it back at me, obviously disgusted.

"Shut up and drink it. It'll heal the burns, and you didn't drink much from me. You need to feed, and there aren't any willing donors here." I threw it back at her and sank my teeth into a bag of my own. She watched me drink for a few seconds, then turned around and tore open her bag. I heard weird slurping sounds, then realized that she didn't know how to use her fangs yet.

"You know you've got fangs, right? They make that a lot easier. It's kinda like a juice box, only you carry your straw with you." She flipped me off over her shoulder, and I watched the skin on her hand return to a more normal deathly pallor. She finished her bag quickly, and I handed her another as soon as she turned around. I dove into my own second bag, trying to replace what she'd taken from me, and handed her a Miller Lite when she was finished.

"You trying to get me drunk?" she asked with a saucy little smirk.

This one was going to be trouble. I could tell. "I couldn't if I wanted to. Not with beer, anyway. It just cuts the aftertaste of the anticoagulants. Now, why don't we start with the easy stuff. What's your name?"

"Abigail Lahey. Pleased to meet you." She held out her hand, and I stared at it for a minute before I burst out laughing. The ridiculousness of the whole night caught up with me right there. From waking up with Sabrina accusing me of murder to fighting in an ambulance to teaching a twenty-something vampire how to drink blood and chase it with cheap beer, it was all too much. I had to reach for a barstool to hold myself up, and that got Greg going, which got Sabrina going, which got Abigail going, until the only one not rolling with laughter was Mike, who looked at us like we'd all been possessed or finally gone insane. Which were both about equally likely, I supposed.

After a few minutes of hysterical laughter, we all settled down in the den. Mike, ever the gentleman, gave up the comfy armchair to Abigail, and I sat on the couch. Sabrina looked at me strangely, then gave a little shrug and sat beside me. Mike brought a straight chair in from the kitchen, while Greg lounged in some bizarre purple beanbag game chair thing with speakers in the butt region. I grabbed a few more beers for everybody, and a Scotch for Mike, then looked Abigail in the eyes. She had pretty eyes; they were a very deep blue. I felt a pang of regret at all the things she was going to miss out on, being dead.

"Now do you believe me? About the whole vampire thing?" I asked gently.

"I think so. I mean, I kinda remember biting you, and I did just drink a couple of pints of blood. That was nasty, by the way."

"That's why I gave you the beer."

"Then there was the whole burning in the sunlight thing, so I guess I believe you. I just…"

"Just what, my child?" Mike asked softly. He had a way of getting people to talk to him. He would have been a good interrogator, but right now he was a pretty good priest, and that was what we needed.

"I keep waiting to wake up, you know?"

"I know," Greg said, a shadow over his expression that I couldn't read. "Believe me, I know."

"Well, unfortunately, you're not going to wake up. This is the new reality for you, Abby. No more sunbathing, no more silver earrings, and a liquid diet forever." I tried to lighten the maudlin mood falling over everyone, to no avail. "But look on the bright side - Goth has never really gone any more out of style than it was to begin with, you'll never get another zit, and you'll never gain weight." I grinned my best lopsided grin, but she just jumped up and ran to the bathroom sobbing.

Sabrina stood to go after her, but I grabbed her arm. "You don't want to do that."

"Why not, Jimmy? The poor girl's obviously in pain."

"She is, but not the kind you're thinking of."

"What are you babbling about now?"

"She's going to want to be alone for a little while as she finishes shuffling off the mortal coil."

"Is there an echo in here? Oh, wait, it's me. *What* are you babbling about?"

"She's gotta puke. A lot. Among other unpleasantries. We don't eat. We don't process food. Do you get the rather disgusting picture? She's barfing up everything she's eaten in the past week and, even if you guys were friends, that's not something you're going to hold somebody's hair back for."

"Oh." Sabrina sat back down on the couch, and we waited for Abigail to finish in the bathroom. About fifteen minutes later, she came out, drained her beer in one long swallow, and got a glass of water from the kitchen.

She walked over to stand in front of the armchair, then looked from Greg to me and back again. "All right, which one of you did this to me? And why? Did you pervs think I'd sleep with you if you made me your little vampire slave? Is that it? Well, let me tell you something, it is *not* going to be like that. I'm not that kind of girl. Um, vampire. Uh...vampiress. You know what I mean. So just 'fess up so I can kick your ass, and we can settle that once and for all."

I looked over at Greg and mouthed "perv?" He shrugged and looked over at Abigail. "Yeah, that's part of the problem. We didn't turn you. And we don't know any other vampires in Charlotte. So we don't know who turned you. Or why. That's why we were at your murder scene, to investigate. It's what we do." He stood and handed her a business card for our firm, Black Knight Investigations. She took it and sat back down in the armchair.

Greg remained standing and started to pace around our very small den, made all the smaller by a vampire of his girth pacing through it. "Did you see who attacked you? Do you remember anything about the assault?"

"I don't remember anything after leaving my chemistry lab. I was walking home and cut through the woods like I always do, making sure to keep my pepper spray handy."

"Yeah," I put in, "safety first." Abigail shot me a hurt look, and Sabrina hit me in the shoulder. Hard. "Sorry," I muttered, rubbing my arm.

"Anyway, the next thing I remember is you with a gun to my head. I don't remember anyone biting me, and I don't remember biting you. Sorry about that, by the way." She looked down, embarrassed.

"No worries. Better me than someone living. At least I managed to fight you off. And the best part is you don't remember it, so I don't even have to apologize for punching you in the head." Sabrina smacked me again, and I quickly added, "But I am sorry about that."

"Don't be. Stuff happens. Now, how do we find the guy that bit me?" she asked, eyes bright with anger.

"How do you know it was a guy?" Greg asked. "Did you remember something?"

"Well, no, but are there other girl vampires around here?" Abigail replied with a shrug.

"Abigail, remember that before a few hours ago we didn't know there were any other vampires around here, male or female. We need to be open to all possibilities," Sabrina said. "Now, are you sure you don't remember anything after leaving class?"

"No, I really don't. I left class, waved goodnight to this cute guy, and turned to go into the woods. Then everything turns gray and hazy."

"She was mojoed." Mike had been uncharacteristically quiet

since getting tossed across the room, but now he interjected his opinion with certainty.

"How do you know?" Sabrina asked. "I mean, it makes sense, but how can you be sure?"

"When the boys first revealed themselves to me, as they were learning of their abilities, they used their power of mental domination on me a few times. It was purely experimental, and consensual on all our parts, just to see what the limits were." Mike quickly put that last bit in when he saw Sabrina about to hit me again. I gave him a grin and motioned for him to continue. "When they ordered me to forget things, it went exactly as Miss Lahey described. Everything went gray around the edges, and my memory just stopped. Then, it picked up later, like an old movie with the middle reel missing."

"So we've got a vamp with mojo. Yeah, that narrows it down." I was getting grumpy, so I stood up and started pacing opposite Greg. The already cramped living room felt downright claustrophobic with my long legs and Greg's jiggly belly vying for airspace. We took turns almost tripping over the coffee table for a couple minutes until something hit me. "Abby, come here."

She walked over to where I stood in the middle of the living room a little hesitantly, so I said, "Calm down, I've already decided not to kill you. Now, stand still." I leaned over to study the bite marks on her neck. Those marks were the last scars she'd ever get. I had found out the hard way that anything up to and including a bullet through the heart would heal without a mark, but the scars that turned us were a reminder of what we used to be. I slid in to within a hair's breadth of her neck and inhaled deeply, trying to get all of her scent into my nostrils. I breathed in her lavender perfume, a hint of my blood, a little sour smell of vomit, the three beers she'd had since waking, and the deep rich smell of the blood I'd given her to feed on. But underneath all those smells, woven into the complex scent of Abby, was another smell, darker, older, and somehow warmer than the others. I knew it was the scent of the vampire who had turned her, and that I'd be able to follow that scent anywhere.

I took a step back, fulfilling my evening's destiny, and falling over the coffee table onto my butt. As I lay sprawled over the table, I flashed back to the last time I'd smelled that very same vampire's scent—the night she had turned me.
*****

I met her at a bar, and she laughed at my jokes. That didn't happen much in the '90s, so I bought her a drink. Then, I bought her another drink. Then, she bought me a drink. Then we danced, which went better than normal. Better than normal meant that I didn't step on her toes too often or fall down on the dance floor. A slow song came on, and the world went away as I buried my face in her neck. I nibbled her earlobe, kissed the side of her neck, and closed my eyes as the scent of fresh flowers filled my nose. She smelled like all the greatest things in the world, all layered over with a hint of sweat and promise.

We left the bar and made our drunken way back to my apartment. The den displayed its normal state of disaster, but she ignored all that. She just stood there amidst the pizza boxes and crushed beer cans and kissed me. When her lips touched mine for the first time, I felt it all the way down to my toes. I heard trumpets, saw fireworks, and lost control of my extremities. She followed me down as I collapsed on the couch, and we made love right there on the living room sofa. She sank her fangs into me as we joined together and killed me with my pants around my ankles and a *Rolling Stone* magazine stuck to my butt.

Her scent charged out of the past and knocked me nearly unconscious fifteen years later in the middle of another messy living room. We had a *problem*.

Chapter 5

"What is it?" Sabrina asked, reaching to help me up. I shook my head and marched over to the liquor shelf in the kitchenette. I poured a double Scotch into a tumbler, looked at it, and turned up the bottle. The peaty amber liquid burned as it went down, and tears sprang to my eyes. I grabbed two beers from the fridge and downed one of them in a long pull. I held the other one to my forehead for a second as I leaned back against the refrigerator. I wasn't flushed; that hadn't happened since Clinton was President but, in times of stress, I sometimes flash back to reflexes from when I was alive.

When I felt I could move without stumbling or twitching like a junkie on day three of withdrawal, I went back over to where the others alternated between aiming panicked looks at me and throwing threatening glares at Abigail. "It's not her," I said, drawing a shaky breath. "Or more to the point, it's not anything she knows about."

"Then what is it, bro?" Greg sounded as solemn as I'd ever heard him and, when I looked, all hints of my dorky, harmless roommate were gone. He had a K-Bar knife in one hand and a pistol in the other. He didn't turn his attention to Abigail when he spoke to me, and I noticed for the first time how scary Greg could be when he wanted that.

"It's her sire. Or dam, or whatever the right word is. It's the scent of the vamp that turned her. I recognize it."

"But you've only ever met two other vamps before tonight, and I'm one of them. And if I didn't turn her... oh, crap." Greg turned away from me and crossed to the door at the bottom of the stairs. He threw the heavy steel door closed and dropped an iron bar across it. Mike and Sabrina shared a concerned look, but said nothing.

"I don't know that we need all that, buddy, but it's not a bad idea." I sat back down on the couch, took a swig of my fresh beer, and put my head in my hands.

"You want to clue the rest of us in on what's got you so freaked out, Jimmy?" Sabrina asked softly. She leaned away a little, as if afraid I might not be in control of myself. Probably a pretty good guess, at that.

"The vamp that turned Abigail. She was the vamp that turned me," I said, looking at the floor. My mind kept going back to that night, a girl way out of my league wanting to dance with me, wanting to leave with me, wanting to go back to my apartment. It was one of the high points of my less than illustrious post-college life, and it ended with her killing me on my couch, and me murdering my best friend. "I'll never forget the smell of her. She smelled like magnolias, and incense, and just a little bit of sweat. It was the best thing I'd ever smelled in my life…" Then, I was off the couch and crouched in front of the toilet, noisily revisiting the beer, Scotch, and a couple of pints of blood. I sat on the tiles retching for a long minute or two before a hand reached in and passed me a glass of water.

I looked up at Mike's face, the face I'd known since we were in elementary school, and wondered where all that gray hair had come from. I took a good look at my friend for the first time in months and saw the yellow tint around his eyes, the sunken cheeks, and the clean-shaven look so different from the neat beard he'd sported since our senior year of high school. Suddenly, everything clicked into place as I sat with the linoleum making flower patterns on my butt and the cool porcelain pressed against my side. "Were you planning on telling me anytime soon?" I whispered low enough that not even Greg could eavesdrop.

Mike twitched a wry smile, and his lips barely moved as he breathed his answer. "I've been trying to figure out the right time."

"What is it? Lung? I know it's not brain; you lack the requisite organ."

He punched me lightly on the arm. "Esophagus. I thought it was acid reflux brought on by chasing you two idiots around all night but, apparently, it was a tumor. The chemo finished up last week, and I'm scheduled for surgery tomorrow. I was actually coming over here to tell you both about it."

"I would hope so, because I was not looking forward to outing you." I looked up at where Greg stood in the doorway, his face solemn. He looked over his shoulder at the living room and continued, "Don't worry, I told the girls it was a private discussion, and I don't think Abigail has figured out that she has bat-ears yet."

"How long have you known?" Mike asked him.

"Since your first treatment. I do the cancer ward thing, remember?"

"What cancer ward thing?" I asked. Apparently, there were all sorts of things going on with my friends that I wasn't aware of.

"I volunteer a couple nights a week hanging with the cancer kids. It's something The Trio got me into."

"I wouldn't have thought those dorks would know there was a world outside their comic shop." I didn't have a very high opinion of the comic shop nerds Greg called The Trio, but they had been useful on a couple of occasions in the past.

"Well, you know Mark, the owner of the shop?" he asked. After my nod, he went on, "Mark's kid brother had leukemia, so I got to know some of the nurses. It was kind of a crappy place, so I took in some games, got them a decent TV, and I go in sometimes and play Xbox with them. You know, let the kids feel like kids for a little while instead of pincushions."

"Wow, Greg. That's really cool. I didn't know anything about it."

"Well, it's kinda my thing, you know. I dunno, a therapist would probably say something about me trying to compensate for having to drink life by helping the sick or something like that. But, I just like to play with the kids. And it seems to help." He looked embarrassed, so I decided to let it drop.

Mike reached over and put a hand on Greg's arm. "I'm sure it helps them quite a bit, my friend. Quite a bit. Now, before the obvious questions arise about a Catholic priest and two vampires in one small room, shall we rejoin the ladies?" We all laughed and, just for a second, it was like we were kids again, then reality came back.

I grabbed Mike's hand for help getting off the bathroom floor. "We'll talk about this a little more, right?" I didn't really mean it as a question.

"Yes. I'll give you all the gory details. And when this is all over, I'll have a nice set of neck scars all my own." He grinned lopsidedly and almost managed to hide the fear in his eyes.

Chapter 6

Sabrina and Abigail were watching the news when we made our way back to the den. Abigail's face was smiling larger than life from the flat screen on the wall.

"Looks like the news has broken," I said, taking my spot on the sofa next to Sabrina.

"Yeah, what are we going to do about it?" Abigail asked. "My parents think I'm dead! They've already been interviewed about finding my body. I want to call them, but she took my cell phone." She glared at Sabrina, who looked pretty unfazed by the girl's anger.

"Good move." I told Sabrina. "Look, pumpkin, I've got a news flash you're not gonna find on WCNC—you *are* dead. You can't call your parents, or your roommate, or your boyfriend, or anyone. They need to move on without you because you're going to have to move on without them. You're a *vampire*. You burn in the sunlight, don't like silver jewelry, have issues with true believers, and have a very, *very* strict liquid diet. If you don't get that through that pretty little head of yours, you will be dead again, this time forever. *Comprende?*" And my grasp of the Spanish language outside of a takeout menu was now exhausted.

She sat there for a minute, staring up at me angrily, then threw her beer bottle at my head and made a dash for the door. Fortunately for her, Greg was really fast for a fat vampire, and he grabbed her after about three steps. She'd be pretty fast, too, once she learned how to make all her limbs work at full speed. But for now, she was easy to control, or at least as easy as an undead coed screaming obscenities in your den could be. Greg put up with her yelling for about thirty seconds longer than I would have, which meant about thirty seconds, and then he crooked a finger at Mike, who followed as he carried her into his bedroom. I heard a muffled *thump* as he dropped the girl on the bed, and he came out, closing Mike in there with the raving girl.

"Is that safe?" Sabrina asked. "Leaving Mike in there with her? She seemed pretty mad."

"Safer than having her out here where Jimmy could stake her," Greg said, grabbing a beer and picking up the wireless mouse and keyboard he kept on the desk in the den. He switched the TV over to computer monitor mode and started surfing the web. "I'm going to spend a little time trying to track our mystery vamp while you two figure out what to do about the ambulance parked behind our house."

I looked over at Sabrina, who looked back at me. "How long do we have before they really start looking for the ambulance? I took off the plates, but I think that might be of limited use, given the conspicuous shape of the vehicle."

"The APB went out right after Bobby made it to the hospital with his story of being carjacked. It helps that we're on the other side of town, and in a cemetery, but we've got to make that thing disappear today."

"How was Bobby?"

"A little shaken up, but also pretty excited. He thinks all this crap is cool."

"We are cool, babe. You know, studly stalkers of the night, protectors of the innocent, sexy predators that all men want to be and all women want to be with." I went for my best rakish look, but Sabrina had collapsed into giggles at "sexy predators."

"Yeah, whatever. You got any clients that run chop shops?"

"No. You got any old informants that owe you a favor?"

"No. So if we're out of the stereotypical ideas, what's next?"

"I sent her an email," Greg said over his shoulder. "She's sending a guy over. Get ten grand out of the safe and put it on the driver's seat. It'll be taken care of in an hour."

"Uh, two questions, buddy. One, we have a safe? And two, who are you talking about?" I watched as Greg got up from his goofy little game chair and went over to the fridge. He pulled it away from the wall to reveal a safe set into the floor underneath it. He dialed a combination and pulled out a wrapped stack of hundred-dollar bills.

He shoved the fridge back into place, dropped the cash in a paper bag, and handed it to Sabrina. "Now, do you really have to ask that second question? Who is the one person we know with fingers into almost every illegal pie in Charlotte?"

Sabrina and I looked at each other and said "Lilith." The immortal seductress had insinuated herself into all sorts of unsavory operations since coming to town as an indentured servant to a fallen angel. When the angel had suddenly became un-fallen, Lilith was stuck here running his operation, and she was not happy about it. She didn't like us very much, but she wasn't usually openly hostile, either. Plus, ten grand bought a lot of tolerance these days, apparently. I decided against asking Greg where the cash had come from. I just chose to pretend he was really good at online poker or something.

Sabrina took the cash upstairs and deposited it on the seat of the ambulance. A little less than an hour later, we heard the rumble of the engine starting and the vehicle pulling away. With that taken care of, we were left to stare at Greg's bedroom door for a little while longer.

Or at least, I stared at the door. Sabrina took a nap, and Greg surfed the web for case information. About an hour into Mike's intervention, Greg waved me over.

"Check this out," he whispered, clicking through a series of web pages faster than I could see them, much less read anything. Ten seconds of that, and I snatched the mouse away from him. I clicked through the tabs, slower, and saw that he'd called up the *Charlotte Observer* online archives as well as somehow having gotten into the paper's internal document storage. I looked through the articles on missing students, then swung Greg's other monitor over. On that screen, he'd hacked into the Charlotte-Mecklenburg Police Department case file database, and he had called up a good twenty missing persons cases.

"Anything look familiar?" he whispered.

"Why are you whispering?" Sabrina asked from over my shoulder, making us both jump.

"Look at this." Greg pointed, drawing our attention to the screens. "Twenty-three students missing over the past eighty years. All seniors or juniors ready to graduate early. All missing after a night class, and no bodies ever found. Sound familiar?"

"Yeah, it sounds like Little Mary Sunshine in there is just the latest in a whole string of vampire kills on campus." I pointed to the case file screen again. "But something's wrong. The last missing person was just six months ago. None of the other attacks have happened within two years of each other."

"So our vampire got careless, so what?" Sabrina asked.

"Careless vampires don't live very long. And they certainly don't live most of a century in one location and then make a stupid mistake like turning someone too close to his last victim. Besides, look at this case." I clicked on another file.

"What about it?" she asked.

"I know two things for a fact. One, the vampire that turned Abby was the same vampire that turned me. I'd know that smell anywhere. And two, I know that she was not in Charlotte when this murder was reported."

"What makes you so sure? I mean, I believe that it smelled like her, but don't some people smell alike?"

Greg and I didn't even hesitate, we both just said "No." My partner, ever the more educational type, explained a little. "Scents are like fingerprints, at least in our experience. No one smells just like someone else. There are a lot of things that go into a person's scent—their ethnicity, their blood type, their geography, their occupation, their diet, their drug uses and abuses, even whether or not they drink regular coffee or decaf. The odds of two people having the exact same scent is so astronomical as to be impossible."

Sabrina's eyes were wide. "I didn't know you got that much out of someone's smell." She looked at me pointedly.

"It can get a little personal if we're not careful, so we don't talk about it. But trust me, when a vampire says he likes the way you smell, it's a pretty huge compliment." She blushed and looked away.

"And how do you know the vampire that turned you wasn't in Charlotte that particular night?" she asked after a minute.

"Because that's the night she killed me in Clemson, almost three hours from here. She didn't have time to do both." I didn't elaborate, and didn't intend to.

"Then we have two vampires working here. The original vampire, who's been hunting on the campus for a long time, and your sire, who has just stepped all over his hunting ground tonight." Greg moved me out of the way and reclaimed his rightful position as master of the mouse.

"Dam," I said quietly.

"What's wrong?" Sabrina asked.

"Nothing, but she's not a sire. Sires are male. She's a dam."

"Like a horse?"

"You know it, missy." I grinned at her, and she blushed, then slapped me on the arm. It was nice to have things back to normal between us, whatever that was. I settled back onto the couch and waited for Mike to talk our newest sibling down off the ledge. It took about three hours of his best counseling, cajoling, and priestly therapy but, when the door opened, he walked out under his own power. Abigail followed meekly behind him, apologizing to all of us as she went to the fridge, grabbed a bag of blood, and joined us around the big screen.

"So what's the plan?" Abigail asked, slurping on the blood. Sabrina looked a little pale, and I reached over with a paper towel and wiped a thin line of blood off the kid's chin.

"You missed a spot."

"Sorry."

"It's okay. You get the technique down over time. For the first few days, though, it's easier to use a straw."

"Huh. Never thought of that."

"Neither did I; Greg came up with it."

"Easy to see who's the brains of the operation, huh?" The kid leaned in a little closer than I was comfortable with, and Sabrina kicked me under the table.

"What?" I asked, sitting up straight.

"Oh, nothing." That woman had an uncanny ability to lower the temperature of a room with just a couple of syllables.

"All right, then. If it's *nothing*, then let's get back to the business at hand. Namely, the sudden one billion percent increase in the known vampire population of Charlotte," Greg said, spinning his chair away from the big monitor to face the rest of us. "Here's what we know. First, Abigail here was turned by the same vampire that turned Jimmy fifteen years ago in a bar outside Greenville, South Carolina. Second, we know there's another vampire that's been turning students for a lot of years, and has been very discrete about it. So, perhaps the vamp that turned you has been working with this other local vampire for some time?"

"Which doesn't make any sense," I said. "This chick is anything but discrete. She didn't hesitate to turn me and, by the way she posed Abigail's body after she drained her, she has no compunction against killing and leaving her victims where they could easily be found. There's no way she's been in Charlotte all this time without us knowing about it."

"I agree," Greg replied. "The third thing we know is that we know very little else. She killed Abigail sometime between eleven PM and two in the morning, and she could have been anywhere from around the corner to Nashville in the time between committing the murder and sunrise."

"She's still here," Abigail said suddenly.

"What do you mean?" I asked.

"I can feel her. She's still close."

"What, like some kind of vampiric radar? Like you're tied to your sire or something?" Greg always used words like *sire* when he got excited. I didn't bother correcting him this time.

"I dunno," the girl said. "I just know she's still close. Like she's not finished with me."

"Maybe she mojoed you before she killed you so you'd know she was close," Sabrina chimed in.

"Can we stop saying she killed me?" Abigail pleaded. "I'm right here, after all."

"Just being precise, dear. You are dead, after all." Sabrina had a snippy tone I'd never heard from her before.

Before the girls escalated things into an all-out catfight, I said, "Why don't we all just get a little rest and go back to the crime scene tomorrow night? We should still be able to pick up any scents or clues then, and with decidedly less risk of spontaneous combustion. Besides, I'm sure the humans in the room aren't the only ones who are starting to drag. Between waking up at stake-point, fighting a newborn, and hijacking an ambulance, it's been a long night."

Sabrina had the good grace to blush a little, and started to gather her things to leave. "Good idea, Jimmy. I'll meet you guys back here around eight tonight. We can figure out where this vamp-factory is hiding out, stake her, and then your little sister can be on her merry way." She pulled on her jacket and holster as I gaped at her.

"Little *sister?*"

"Well, yeah. After all, you two were made by the same vamp, so doesn't that make her your sister?" She flashed me a vicious grin and headed up the stairs. The more I hung out with her, the more confused I was as to exactly which one of us had the fangs.

Greg rolled in his chair a little until she leaned back around the stairs and said, "So what does that make her to you, Greg? Your aunt?" He fell out of his chair with a thwack, like a side of beef hitting the carpet, kind of wet and fleshy. Mike smiled and followed Sabrina up the stairs.

"If you two comedians are done, I'm going to bed," I said, heading toward my room.

"Uh, where am I supposed to sleep? Should I have a coffin or something?" Abigail stood in the middle of the den looking confused and a little scared.

"Nah, there's an air mattress in the coat closet, and the couch pulls out," Greg said, demonstrating the convertible sofa. "You've seen the shape of my room, and Jimmy's is much, much worse, so trust me when I say this is the safest place for you to sleep."

"But what if somebody comes in and tries to stake me in my sleep?" She was starting to shake a little, and I felt something I hardly ever felt—sympathy.

"Okay, look," I said. "We'll all camp out in here for the night. It'll be fine." I dragged my mattress onto the floor and plopped it down between the stairs and the couch. I went to the closet and deposited my shotgun beside the mattress. "There. Now anything coming in the door will have to get through me, and my little friend." My best Pacino impression was pretty bad, but it got a smile out of her. Greg dropped his mattress on the other side of the couch, between the den and the kitchen, effectively barricading our guest in the general vicinity of the sofa.

She looked around at the arrangement and settled in on the couch. "Thanks, guys. I'm just a little scared, you know?"

"I know," Greg answered from the floor. "It's been a while, but I remember what it's like to wake up dead. It's a scary thing, but we're here for you."

"Just in case," Abigail said, as I turned off the last of the lights and settled in for a quick snooze. "Can I have a gun?"

"No!" Greg and I shouted in unison.

Chapter 7

I awoke with a tickling sensation under my nose and resisted the urge to sneeze. I shook my head, trying to figure out what it was. I pried one eye open, saw a veil of yellow across my vision, and became even more confused. I took a deep breath and stretched, or tried to. I realized that my face was covered in hair, and there was something laying on my arm. A half-second later, I realized that the some*thing* was a some*one*, and exactly who it was.

"Oh, crap!" I whispered, as I sat bolt upright, dumping Abigail off of my arm, off the mattress, and onto the floor. I looked around the room and saw Sabrina sitting in the armchair drinking a soda and staring at me with eyes full of hurt.

"This isn't what you're thinking!" I blurted, trying to disentangle myself from the blankets and the blonde. I eventually stumbled to my feet.

"And what am I thinking, James? Are you suddenly psychic on top of your other *gifts*? And what business is it of mine if you fall into bed with the first cold body that comes along? After all, I have no claim on you. So what do I care?" Her tone of voice said she was unconcerned and didn't have a care in the world, but her pounding heartbeat said she was a hair's breadth away from shooting me in the face.

Greg had woken up at the noise and, in a fuzzy sleep-haze, was looking between Sabrina, me, and the blonde lump on the floor that was Abigail. "What's going on?"

"Shut up," Sabrina and I said in unison.

"Oh," Abigail said from the floor. "Sorry. I got scared in the middle of the day and crawled in bed with you. I hope that's okay." She cocked a sleepy and sultry pose from the floor, and I knew she was going to be trouble.

I stalked over to Sabrina in my t-shirt and boxers, hair haystacked all over the place like a porcupine on a bender, and pulled her to her feet. I looked the furious detective square in the face and said, "I don't know exactly what's going on between us, and I don't think you do, either. But I know this—you matter to me. You matter more to me than any person has since I've been dead, and I will not do anything to screw that up. I don't have a whole lot going for me. I'm skinny with bad hair and a big nose. I've been dead since Clinton was in the White House, and I can't ever go on long walks in the sunlight with anyone again. I can't write poetry or play music, and I have dietary restrictions that make veganism look easy. But I am one thing above all else—I am loyal. I don't have many friends, or whatever we are, in my life, and I will fight past death to keep the ones that I have. So if you're pissed at me, fine. Be pissed. I earn that a couple dozen times a day. But if you think for one second that I would ever do anything to hurt you, then you better think again, Detective."

Then I kissed her. I grabbed her face in both my hands and I kissed her like my life depended on it. Which, given the kind of stake she'd been carrying last night, it might have. She stiffened at first but, after a second, she put an arm around me and kissed me back, and it was the greatest feeling I'd had in all the years I'd been dead. After a long minute, she pulled back, and I saw one tear rolling down her right cheek. I reached up with my index finger and wiped it away. "No more of that." I pulled her to me for a tight hug. I could have sworn in that moment that I felt some of her warmth leach into me and push away the cold for just a second, then it was gone.

"Well, then," Sabrina said. "I suppose we'll talk more later. But we've got a few things to do first. One, put some clothes on; we've got a crime scene to check out."

"What's two?" Greg asked, heading toward his room and a shower.

"Two is this." Sabrina walked over to Abigail and leaned in very close. She whispered too low for even Greg and me to eavesdrop, but I saw Abigail turn a couple of shades paler as she listened. After a long moment, the dark-haired detective leaned back and looked deep into the blond vampire's eyes. Abigail looked back, swallowed deeply, and nodded. Just to make things even more surreal, Abigail then threw her arms around Sabrina's neck and hugged her fiercely before getting to her feet and running to the bathroom.

"What was all that?" I asked, as Sabrina came back to my side.

"The facts of life. I don't think she's ever had very many girlfriends, so I explained the way the world worked."

"Is that all?"

"That and I told her if I ever found her playing all snuggly with you again that I'd stake her and leave her in the middle of Panthers Stadium to watch the sunrise." She gave me a little kiss on the cheek, and said "Now, go get cleaned up. You've got evening breath."

A quick shower and fang-brushing later, we were back at the big hole on campus. According to Sabrina, she'd gotten a ton of pressure from the upper floors of the Charlotte-Mecklenburg Police

Department to release the crime scene so that the city's latest construction jewel could move forward, but she had managed to buy us one more night to poke around. That meant anything we wanted to collect had to be gathered right now because any trace evidence would be gone come sunrise.

"I don't get it," Abigail said, as we got out of Sabrina's unmarked car at the crime scene. "Weren't the CSI guys or whatever here already?"

"They were," I answered. "But we have a few resources they're lacking."

"Like what?"

"Like a super-sniffer that knows what it's looking for," Greg replied, jumping down into the foundation where we'd found Abigail's body less than twenty-four hours before. I followed him down the vampire way and grinned a little at Abigail and Sabrina carefully picking their way through the red dirt and rocks.

"You could jump, you know. I'll catch you," I yelled up at them.

Sabrina looked up and shot me the finger, while Abigail responded, "You'd enjoy it too much!"

A few minutes later, we congregated in the bottom of the construction site. Greg took Abigail off to one side to give her a lesson on her newly enhanced senses, and to get her away from the place where we had found her corpse, while I started sniffing around the actual crime scene. It took a few moments to separate the scents of diesel fuel, mud, and hydraulic fluid, but after I zeroed in on the location where she had been drained, I found the trail almost immediately. The spot was a couple of yards away from where the body had been staged, and there was just one tiny drop of blood in the dirt to mark it. I stood still, breathing deeply. A second later, the scent of *her* flooded my nostrils and set me on fire like cheap moonshine, burning away everything else. I smelled lilacs, swamp water, and a hint of rot under the hot scent of fresh blood and vamp saliva. The hair on the back of my neck stood as I locked onto the trail and followed it up the steepest part of the excavation. When I got to the top of the pit, I turned and looked back, taking advantage of the perfect image below. The slab of concrete where we had found Abigail was beautifully lit by the full moon, just like it would have been last night. I closed my eyes and imagined the girl lying there, posed as if she looked up at where I now stood.

"Sacrifice," I murmured. Greg's head popped up.

"What?" he whispered back to me across a hundred yards of construction debris.

42

"She was an offering to something. I don't know what, but she wasn't just turned and left here. She was meant as an offering."

"Interesting theory, little vampire. However did you get so smart?" purred a low voice from directly behind me. I jumped a little and pinwheeled my arms to keep from going head over heels back into the pit. I whirled around once I'd caught my balance to find a short woman in leather pants and a sheer black top standing behind me smirking. Her dark hair was pulled back in a severe ponytail, and a spiked leather collar and thigh-high boots completed the dominatrix look perfectly. I didn't need super-senses to know she wasn't wearing anything under that top, and the patent leather pants were so tight she must have had more super-powers than I'd known about to get into them. That image, coupled with a scent somewhere between cinnamon, sex, and cotton candy swirled together and made me stupider than usual whenever the oldest hottie in the known universe was around.

"What are you doing here, Lilith?" I growled.

"The same thing you are. Trying to find out why there's suddenly another vampire running around in my city," she said calmly.

"Your city? Aren't you still the new demoness on the block?" I asked archly.

"So judgmental, little vampire. And after I helped you with your little ambulance problem, too." She stepped closer, and even my dead heart sped up a little. Lilith was sexy before a word even existed for it, and she made me seriously uncomfortable. After all, anyone who could answer "boxers or briefs" about the original Adam had some serious magic. And did I mention she was wearing a sheer black top with nothing else? I might be dead, but I'm not *dead*.

"Yeah… um, thanks for that. Now what do you know about this new vamp?" I circled around Lilith to put her back to the big hole in the ground. I figured it best to limit my obvious threats to one at a time. I could usually avoid falling in big holes, or I could avoid getting into a fight with immortal hotties, but I wasn't sure about my ability to do both at the same time.

"I know even less than you do, Mr. Black, and I promise you those are words I never thought I would hear myself say." Lilith took a step over the edge and floated down into the pit to stand beside the concrete altar where Abigail had been sacrificed.

"Nice trick," I said, jumping down to land beside her in a puff of gray concrete dust. The others joined us, but Sabrina hung back a little. Her last meeting with Lilith had been a little contentious and, for once, she showed that discretion was in her vocabulary. "Now," I went on. "What do you know? Or sense? Or guess?"

Lilith walked up to Abigail and sniffed around her for a few seconds, looking carefully at the scars on her throat. She even leaned in and licked the side of the girl's neck, which I was sure sent Greg to a happy place, but it just creeped me out a little. "I sense nothing out of the ordinary. I know nothing about this vampire at all, except that she made both you and the young one here." I didn't give her the satisfaction of asking her how she knew; I just nodded for her to go on.

"In the ancient days when monsters were entering the territory of another, stronger beast they would leave a peace offering where it would be easy to find. A sacrifice, if you will, to request safe passage. Perhaps that is what you were, my dear."

"I was an offering?" Abigail sputtered, outraged.

"Looks like it, kiddo. Now we need to find out to who," I said.

"To whom, little vampire, to whom. And while I would normally suggest that I would be the logical choice, this is not the place to make a sacrifice to my authority. And I have little use for the Sanguine. So I suspect that you are looking for someone else as the intended recipient of your lovely sister."

"Don't you mean *we* are looking for someone else, Lilith?" I asked.

"Oh no, little vampire. There is no *we*, royal or otherwise, in this equation. Now that I am fairly certain that this involved me not at all, I shall remove myself from the fray. If you require my assistance at any point, you know where to find me. And you are always *very* welcome." Lilith stroked a hand down my chest, grinned at Sabrina, then floated back up to the lip of the construction site and walked away. A few seconds later, I heard a motorcycle rev up and drive away.

I wondered for a second why I hadn't heard her drive up until Greg said, "She was waiting for us, bro."

"Huh?" I grunted, studiously not looking at where Lilith had just gone and even more studiously trying not to think about how *warm* her hand had been on my chest. That woman made me more uncomfortable than most, and that's saying something.

"I didn't hear her drive up, and I was paying attention. She was waiting for us. I'd guess she came out here during the day, got whatever information she was going to get, and waited for us to show up to tell us it wasn't her deal."

"Um… for the new kid, who was that?" Abigail actually raised her hand to ask the question.

"That was Lilith. Rumored to be the first wife of Adam. Yeah, that Adam. She was banished for wanting to be on top, and Eve came along afterward. Theoretically, she was made from the same dirt Adam was, thus had the silly idea that men and women should be equals. That led to the whole thing about creating Eve from a rib so women would forever be subservient to men, and we see how well *that's* worked out for everyone. So Lilith is an immortal, and there are rumors about her being a succubus, a demoness, and a host of other unpleasant things. And she's kinda the Kingpin of Charlotte, if you've read enough *Daredevil* comics to get the reference." Greg had put on his best professor tone for his answer, and I could have sworn he actually got a little taller while pontificating.

"I saw that really crappy movie with Ben Affleck, if that's what you mean. But I get it. What does she do?"

"Owns a strip club, launders money, runs hookers, disposes of stolen ambulances, whatever pays the bills," Sabrina chimed in, distaste dripping off her tongue.

"And you guys don't like her?" Abigail asked.

"*Despise* is a better choice," Sabrina answered.

"Yeah, despise works," Greg said quickly.

"Not me, I'm just afraid of her," I said. Abigail looked at me, confused. "I'm afraid of anyone and anything I can't kill. And Lilith tops the list in Charlotte, so I'm scared gutless by her. I try not to let it get in the way of occasionally having to work with her, though."

"I don't get it," Abigail went on. "Why did she come out here just to tell us that she wasn't responsible for... turning me?"

"Lilith is above all else a businesswoman. She loves few things in this world, but money is high on the list. And if we go in and start making a mess of her club, then that costs her money. She knows we'll probably believe her if she tells us the truth, so that saves her money and saves us time. It's a win-win. And I did just give her ten grand for a five grand disposal job, so she probably looks at this little info-dump as keeping her books square." Greg ticked off the points on his fingers as he spoke, and I looked at my conniving little partner with respect.

"Well, if Abby wasn't a sacrifice to Lilith, then who?" Sabrina asked.

"That's why we're detectives, I guess. I lost the scent of the vamp when she got into a car at the top of the pit, but I caught something else odd up there. Greg, come with me. You two keep checking for physical evidence. Abby, this will be a good test for

45

your vamp-vision."

"What am I supposed to do?" Sabrina asked.

"I dunno, Detective. Teach her to detect?" With that, I turned around and bounded up the side of the pit in a couple of jumps, my pudgy partner right on my heels.

Chapter 8

"What are we looking for?" Greg asked at the top of the hole.

"Take a good whiff." I gestured to the woods near the site.

Greg walked over to the trees separating the stadium site from the apartments just off campus and took a deep breath. He doubled over, coughing with the intensity of the smell. Sometimes I forgot that Greg's sense of smell was much stronger than mine. This wasn't one of those times; I'd just really wanted to hit him over the head with my discovery.

"Holy crap!" he gasped when he was able to speak again.

"Yeah. Now what is it?"

"What are *they*, to be precise. There are two distinct scents here, both from last night."

"Okay," I said, trying to keep my patience. "What. Are. They?"

"Well, there's the scent of vamp, a bunch of them, and at least one of them is really old."

"How can you tell?" I sniffed the air experimentally, but couldn't find anything that told me if any vamp was old or young.

"You know how blood smells after it's been sitting on the counter for a few days?"

"Boy, do I, and I've been meaning to talk to you about taking out the trash a little quicker."

Greg cut me off with a wave of his hand. "Later. Well, this is the same thing. Abby smells like fresh blood because she's a new vamp. You and I don't. Lilith smells even older, even though she's not a vamp. I think it's got something to do with the tissue, or how we maintain our life force or something."

"Anyway," I threw in quickly before Greg got too far down the rabbit hole with his theorizing. "So several vamps, at least one old one. What's the other thing? That thing that smells like a cross between cheap cigars and wet dog?"

"I have no idea, man. I've never smelled anything like it." He edged further into the woods and sniffed deeply.

"Like what?" Sabrina asked from behind me.

I jumped about seven feet in the air and whirled around on her. "Woman, I swear I'm going to put a bell on your neck!"

"Try it. We'll see where that bell ends up. Never smelled anything like what?"

"We don't know," Greg said from the woods.

"Well, what about all these vampires I smell?" Abigail asked, causing me to jump again.

"Dammit, would you two cut that out!" After I calmed down, I said, "I don't know what we're going to do about the vamps, but we can't do it tonight."

"Why not?" Sabrina asked.

"Not enough guns and too many potential appetizers in the party." I gave her my best "don't argue with me" look. She took the hint, which kind of amazed me.

"Fine," she said. "Then you should at least reconnoiter their location so we can get back there when we're better prepared. It's supposed to rain tomorrow, and that'll wash away any scents they've left behind."

"How do you know that?" I asked. "It's not like you have a super-sniffer of your own."

"There are these mythical creatures, Jimmy, called dogs. We in the police department sometimes work with these creatures to apprehend bad people called criminals. So we spend a lot of time in a great place of learning called the Academy, so we can study these creatures and how best to use them." She spoke very slowly, as if to a particularly stupid child, which I supposed was somewhat fair. Abigail covered her mouth with one hand, but Greg didn't even bother to hide his belly laughs. I shot them both the finger and walked off into the woods to follow the vamps' scent.

I motioned for Greg to stay behind because he's about as stealthy as an epileptic rhinoceros. I also hoped that he'd be able to keep Abigail back there as well. If I was going to go stalking a nest of vampires, I didn't need a rookie looking over my shoulder. I lost the scent a couple of times, but had watched enough bad survival movies to track in concentric circles until I picked it up again.

After sneaking through the woods for about half an hour, I came to a tall fence around a Victorian-style house complete with porch pillars. It looked like a cross between *The Amityville Horror* and the frat house from *Animal House*, with peeling paint, loose shutters, and a parking lot full of stereotypical college beaters in the front. The scent trails ran up to and over the fence line, so the vampires must have gone into the house. I decided I didn't want to take on a dozen or more vampires by myself, so I settled for watching the house instead.

I eyeballed the place for about fifteen minutes and saw no hint of movement inside. Nothing flickering past a window, no glow of a TV, no sounds of rampant teenage fornication, nothing. I made a mental note of where I was relative to campus and the major roads, then crept back to the others.

"Well?" Sabrina asked, when I got back to where they were waiting by the car.

"Deep subject," I replied. "Let's go get something to eat, and I'll tell you all about it."

"You don't eat," she shot back.

"Yeah, I do, and the cupboard's pretty bare. So let's go visit Bobby and do a little grocery shopping. I'll fill you in on the way to the hospital."

"Bobby's out sick today. Stress from last night's *attack* and all. What's your Plan B for dinner?" She looked a little nervous at the question.

"You don't want to know. Take Greg home. Abby and I will catch a ride." I got out of the car.

"Oh, no," Greg said. "She comes with me. I am not going to have you teaching her how to hunt. Not this early."

"We don't have a choice. She hunts, or you do. There are four pints in the fridge, just enough for one of us for one night. Now you can keep your morality, or you can keep Abby all lily-white, but you can't do both. Abby, how do feel about takeout?"

"Well…" The girl looked down at her feet for a second, then back up at me with a grin. "We are the top of the food chain, right?"

"Exactly." I looked at Greg and Sabrina, who looked alternately disturbed and disappointed. "We'll be home in an hour. Two at the most, I promise. Then I'll fill you all in on what I found at the end of the vamp trail, and we can make plans for our next move."

I moved closer to Sabrina, and said quietly, "And we've got a few things to chat about, I think." She blushed a bit, but nodded and gave me a quick kiss on the cheek before she got in the car and drove off with Greg.

I looked at Abigail, the very image of youth and innocence, and actually felt a twinge of guilt before I put my conscience back into its lead-lined box and said, "All right, kiddo. You ready to learn how to be a vampire?

"The best thing about a college campus is the variety. It's like a buffet for vampires, if you look at it in the right way. You've got young, old, boy, girl, all the ethnicities and dietary preferences. And all of those things affect the taste of the blood," I explained in a whisper as we walked. We weren't even walking together, more like twenty feet apart but, thanks to our vamp senses, Abigail had no trouble hearing me. "Personally, I prefer my snacks to be a little on the heavy side and over legal drinking age. I also shoot for the healthy-looking meals, but nothing that smells like a vegan. I didn't care much for carrot juice when I was alive, so it's not really on my menu nowadays. Now I'll feed first, and you can watch how it's done. Then, it'll be your turn."

"O-okay," Abigail whispered. I felt the tension coming off of her even from a few yards away. I thought back to my early days as a vampire. It sure would've been nice to have had somebody with a little experience to show me the ropes, instead of having to figure it all out with Greg, who only had his Anne Rice library and a string of bad movies to draw from. There had been a lot of mistakes along the way, ranging from hilarious to downright terrifying, and I was determined to make things a little easier on Abby. I realized with a start that I was beginning to feel protective of her, like she really was my little sister.

I spotted my dinner coming out of the theatre building, one of my favorite spots on any college campus. The tech students were generally there until all hours. They usually started off pretty pale and had a predilection for turtlenecks that made my life a lot simpler. I picked a girl of about twenty with long, dark hair and blue eyes. She was tapping away on her iPhone when I stepped out of the shadows. She whipped up her little can of pepper spray lightning-quick, but locked eyes with me before she started spraying. That was her last mistake of the night.

"Put that away," I put the force of my will behind my words. Her eyes glazed over, and the pepper spray went back into her purse.

"Come with me," I continued, and she followed me into the woods between the theatre building and the visitors parking deck. I led her off the path a couple of yards and had her sit with her back to a tree. She wasn't beautiful by any stretch, but had a striking air about her. I sat next to her and chatted idly about the weather for a moment before I leaned into her and bit deeply into her carotid artery. Hot blood splashed the back of my throat, and my eyes rolled back in my head. The coppery taste was something I could live without, frankly, but the hot sensation of life pouring down my throat was something I'd never been able to explain.

It was like everything about the person was flowing into me, like I was drinking their dreams, their hopes, their very soul. It was a better rush than anything I ever felt while alive and, every time I took a victim, I understood a little better why some vampires went nuts and did it all the time. But I also understood why Greg tried so hard to stay off the vein, because it was harder to go back to the bag after every fresh meal.

I knelt there, letting the visceral pleasure of drinking from the source wash over me for a couple of seconds before I forced myself back to reality. I drank for several minutes, taking about three pints from the girl before I felt like I could sustain myself for a night or two. When finished, I took a moment to lick the last drops from her neck and watch as the vamp saliva healed the puncture wounds almost immediately.

I looked in her eyes, and she stared back at me glassily. I'd drained her just to the brink of unconsciousness and felt a twinge of guilt about that. I'd fed more than usual, but the past couple of nights had taken a lot out of me. I'd had more close calls in twenty-four hours than I usually had in a week, leaving me with a distinct sense that my life wasn't going to get any less complicated in the near future. "When you wake up, you won't remember me. You'll remember drinking too much and lying down here to rest for just a minute. Now sleep." She obediently rolled onto her side and began to breathe evenly among the pine needles.

"Will she be okay out here all night?" Abigail asked.

"I checked the weather. It's supposed to be unseasonably warm tonight. Lows in the sixties, so yeah, she'll be fine. No one will notice her out here, and she'll wake up in the morning a little dizzy and maybe a touch embarrassed, but none the worse for wear. Now, let's find you some dinner."

We wandered the campus for almost another hour before Abigail found somebody she wanted to bite. It was like taking a picky eater to an all-you-can-eat Chinese buffet and having them order chicken fingers. I mean, really, what was the point? But she finally found a guy she liked in a parking deck over by the student center and mojoed him into the back seat of his Suburban, although, I wasn't sure if she needed any mojo for that. She was pretty cute, after all. She even made out with the guy for a few minutes before he made some comment about cold hands, and then she bit him. I watched her back stiffen when she got her first taste of fresh blood, and it was almost like her hair stood on end. She drank from the guy for a minute or two, then I reached in and tapped her on the shoulder.

No response. I grabbed her shoulder and shook her. Still nothing. I leaned into the back seat with a growl and grabbed a fistful of her blond hair. I yanked, and she finally came free, glaring at me with fangs bared.

"Hungry!" she demanded, voice low and threatening.

"Stupid," I replied, my own voice very calm and very flat. Either my word or my tone registered with her, and reason came back into

51

her feral eyes.

"Is it always like that?" she asked quietly.

"Yeah, every time. It gets easier to know when to say when, though. And sometimes you'll find someone who ate something that disagrees with you, but most of the time it's pretty awesome."

"So why do you drink out of the bag? That stuff tastes like crap. I can't imagine drinking that plastic-tasting junk after what I just had."

"We drink out of the bag because we can't hunt every night, or even every couple of nights, and stay hidden. And staying hidden is pretty important when you're as allergic to sunlight as we are." I didn't go into all the moral implications with her. It didn't feel like the right time.

"And you're afraid you'll like it too much and turn into the monster you think you are?"

I hated perceptive women, and now fate had dropped another one into my life. "Something like that. Now clean up and juice him into forgetfulness. We've gotta get home."

She wiped the blood off her chin, and then looked around, confused. "How exactly are we going to do that? You sent Sabrina and Greg off with the car."

"You're in a car, aren't you?"

"Yeah, but he's out like a light."

"Then he won't mind if we borrow it, will he?" I reached into the guy's pocket, grabbed his keys, and got behind the wheel.

"What about when he wakes up in a cemetery?" Boy, she was just full of questions.

"Then you mojo him into thinking he was at a party, and we toss a few empty beer bottles into his car for a reminder. And it'll get some of the garbage out of the house. Kill two birds with one stone." I grinned as I backed the monstrous SUV out of the parking space and headed home.

Chapter 9

It was almost dawn by the time we ditched the car a couple blocks from the cemetery, got home, and caught everyone up on the vamp nest I'd found. We emailed a summary of the night's activities to Mike and asked him to meet us at our place after sundown, figuring if there were a lot of vampires around, a priest and a cop were about the only flavor of humans we were willing to take in with us. Sabrina headed home for a couple hours' sleep, and the rest of us trundled off to our respective rooms, with the sofa for Abby.

I felt the sun setting as I awoke to a sense of pressure against my temple. I opened my eyes to see a large hairy man who smelled of cheap cigars holding a pistol to my temple and leaning far too close to my face for comfort. I was getting pretty tired of waking up with unexpected people in my bed and, while I didn't mind so much waking up beside Sabrina or Abby, the huge bearded man with a .357 at my temple was a definite drop in the quality of bedmates.

"Give me one good reason not to splatter your brains all over the comforter, you blood-sucking parasite," he growled, and I got a much better look at his slightly pointed canines than I needed.

"Because I'm a blood-sucking contributing member of society? I mean, really, I pay taxes and everything." He growled again, and I heard the cocking of the pistol.

"Okay," I tried again. "How about because I have a Glock 19 pointed at your testicles and can pull the trigger at least once before you can get a round through my head?"

"Won't kill me, blood-sucker. Unless you're packing silver rounds, which I doubt." He leaned back a little, though, and looked down to see that I did in fact have a pistol aimed straight at his most prized possessions.

"I don't think I care, pal. You ever had to regrow your balls? I bet it hurts like the devil. And it's really about the suffering when you're shooting somebody's nuts off, anyway. So why don't you get off me, go wait in the den, and I'll come join you for a beer after I take a leak?"

"You're awfully calm for somebody with a gun in his face." He hadn't moved yet, but I was pretty sure he was about to, which was good, because he was heavy, and making me have to pee. And I was really starting to dislike the smell of wet fur.

"That's because," came Greg's voice from the doorway, "he knows I've got you covered, and my shotgun *is* loaded with silver slugs. Now, get up, and let's go to the den." The guy got off of me, holstered his pistol, and left my bedroom under my partner's watchful eye. I headed to the bathroom thinking about the new security system we were totally going to have to install.

I took care of nature's rather urgent call and joined Greg and our unexpected guest in the den. They were standing over the couch, looking down at Abigail's sleeping form. She had her hands folded across her chest in a funereal pose, and a placid expression on her face. "All she's missing is a lily in her hands," I said, as I grabbed the back of the couch.

"Wake up, Sleeping Beauty!" I tipped the couch far enough to dump the kid onto the floor. Her pink panty-clad rump with "Tuesday" written on it in purple letters pointed up at the sky for a few seconds before she whirled the blankets around herself and shot into the bathroom at top vamp speed. Laughing, I sat down on the sofa and tossed a beer at our guest.

He raised his monobrow briefly before twisting off the top and plopping down in the armchair. "Thanks," he grumbled. He was obviously a little put out at my lack of fear, but I wasn't giving him any answers until he gave me a few first.

Greg took up his post in the game chair and glared at the intruder drinking our best domestic swill. "Okay, now would you like to explain who you are and what you're doing here?"

"I'd rather not, but that's probably not an option at this point, is it?" tall, dark, and hirsute answered.

"Probably not, furball." I replied before Greg could get a word in. That eyebrow shot up again, and he tipped his beer at me.

"So you know."

"I do, but I don't think Greg does."

"How?"

"You're not the only one with a nose that works."

"Know what?" my behind-the-times partner asked.

"See?" I said.

"I do," the werewolf in my den answered. "My name is Kyle King. I'm a private investigator working on a series of odd murders all over the Southeastern U.S. I followed the trail of bodies to Charlotte and picked it up last night at the university. That trail led me to you two, and here I am."

"Wow," I pronounced grandly. "That is a true marvel of understatement, Mr. King. Shall I point out just a few of the things that you may have neglected to mention? There was the fact that the trail you followed here didn't exactly lead to us, but rather to the very mobile young lady in our bathroom. There's the fact that murders are investigated by the police, you know, people with actual authority and jurisdiction? Then there's the fact that you didn't follow our trail by any ordinary means, but rather by your prodigious sniffer. And last, but not least, there's the fact that you couldn't come visit us last night because you were too busy scratching fleas and chasing cars under the full moon to focus on anything else. Isn't that right, Mr. King?"

"I don't chase cars. And I don't have fleas, bloodsucker." He stood up from his chair and stalked over to me. I stood up at the same time and got in his face, while Greg sat on the couch ticking off the new ideas on his fingers. So much for him being the smart one.

"Wait a minute!" Greg yelled, bouncing up and interposing his gut between King and me. "You're a *werewolf*?"

"Yeah," King muttered, sitting back down.

"That is so *cool*!" Greg did that annoying thing where he bounced up and down on his heels again, so I took the opportunity to go get another couple of beers. Abigail came out of the bathroom while I was at the fridge, and I waved her back into my bedroom.

"Bite me. I want my pants," she said in the tone of a pretty girl who was used to all the guys gawking when she walked across the room. And I had to admit, the sight of her walking across the room in just her panties and a t-shirt was pretty gawk-worthy. *Note to self*, I thought. *Get her some more clothes. Like burlap*.

As she was pulling on her pants and giving Greg the closest thing to heart palpitations he'd felt in a decade and a half, King looked her up and down, and asked, "Are you Abigail Lahey?"

"Yep." She held out her hand. "Pleased to meet you. And you are?"

He stood and shook her hand. "Kyle King. I was informed that you were dead. Apparently, someone was mistaken."

"Not really. I'm pretty dead. Feel how cold my hands are?" She laughed as King jerked his hand back. "What's the matter? You were perfectly willing to accept that the boys were vampires, why not me?"

"I saw you. I mean, you were at the college." Abigail had done exactly what I'd hoped she would do; she'd rattled King into giving us more information than he intended. I decided that was time for me to jump in.

"Yeah, about that," I said, head still in the fridge. "Was that before or after she was left as a peace offering to the local vamp warren?" One of these days, I was going to have to figure out the correct name for a group of vamps. Were we a pride? A nest? A clutch? Who even knew those things?

"She was dead when I got there, bloodsucker. I don't kill people." King settled back in the chair.

"No, you don't. You just hump their legs and pee on their tires." I tossed beers to him, Abigail, and Greg. "Are you old enough to drink, Abby?"

"I'm dead. I think it's okay. And yes, I'm twenty-one." She flicked the bottle cap at me. I caught it and tossed it in the general vicinity of the trashcan.

"Twenty-one forever. I can think of worse fates." King said.

Greg and I just stared at him with flat looks that clearly said, "You have no idea what you're talking about."

"So, King. Why are you here?" King started to say something, but I cut him off. "Yeah, yeah, I know the whole line about murders and chasing the killers, but why are you *here*? Or if you want to get real specific about it, why are you here instead of hunting down the vamp that killed Abby? Or at least chasing down the coven of vampires at the school?" Still having trouble with the designation, I just decided to run through all of them until I figured out the best name for a bunch of vampires.

"I saw you at the crime scene and did a little research. Sounds like you lumps are actually pretty good at what you do, no matter how stupid you look." I let that pass, but Greg got an indignant look on his face. I'd warned him about the spandex for years, but sometimes he just had to hear it from somebody outside the family. "I can't take this vampire chick on my own; I've tried. And if I can't take out one vamp, there's no way I can take out the dozen or so that are hanging around campus. I checked with a couple of folks around town, and everybody says you're square. So I came here for help."

"You've got a peculiar way of asking, buddy." I wasn't quite ready to let go of the whole waking up with a gun in my face thing.

"I jumped to a couple of different conclusions when I saw Miss Lahey lying on your couch. Sorry about the gun." He actually looked a little contrite, so I figured I'd give him the benefit of the doubt.

"Fine. Sorry about threatening to shoot off your junk." I leaned over, and we clinked beer bottles, sealing the apology according to the guy code.

"You threatened to shoot off his... you know?" Abigail asked, suppressing a giggle.

"Yeah, I've had a whole string of unusual awakenings this week, so I've taken to sleeping with a pistol. I heard Chief Howls-at-Moon here when he came through the door upstairs, so I was ready for him when he got to my room."

"Why didn't you just stop him in the den?" she asked.

"I wanted to control the situation, and the smaller room worked in my favor. I'm better in close quarters because I'm skinny and can navigate better than he can. Plus, I know where all the crap on the floor is in my room, and there's no telling where Greg left an Xbox controller in the den for me to trip on."

"Good point. I found three buried in the couch, along with an Apple TV remote."

"I've been looking for that!" Greg jumped up to grab the slim silver cylinder from her.

"Well, King. This is your vamp-hunt. What's the plan? Who do we go after first, the one who made Abby or the bunch hanging out at the college smoking weed and eating cold pizza with B-Negative?" I knew that whatever the plan, I wasn't going to like it at all.

Chapter 10

I was right, I hated the plan from the second tall, dark, and fuzzy started with, "We should split up to cover more ground."

"Seriously?" I asked, shocked right out of my fangs. "You're a werewolf, and you've never even seen a horror movie? Do you know what happens when the good guys split up? Nothing good, that's what!"

"I hate to agree with my partner, but it is kinda typical of the genre. The good guys split up and no matter who the camera follows, they end up needing exactly the item or skill that's with the other team," Greg said, nodding.

"Yeah, it's one of the cardinal rules of horror flicks. There's a monster hiding right where the cat just jumped out from, the virgin always lives, and you never, ever split up. So we stick together," I said with finality.

"Then how do you expect to gather intel on the operations of the vampires at the school while we chase down your sire and separate her head from her body?" King asked.

"We do one, then the other. The college vamps have been there for a long time and, if they're anything like the college kids I knew, they're probably stoned. So they'll still be there, with the munchies, when we get back," I said.

"Back from where?" Sabrina said, as she came down the stairs.

"Wasn't expecting you here this early," I greeted her. "You get any sleep?"

"I'll sleep when I'm dead." She tossed an empty energy drink can into my recycle bin.

"Not necessarily," Abigail said. "Looks like tonight we chase more dead people, but this time we get to bring a bloodhound!"

"I'm not a bloodhound," the surly werewolf groused.

"Detective Sabrina Law, meet Kyle King. He's another private investigator looking into a string of murders all over the South. Abby here seems to be the latest victim." I made the best introductions I could as Sabrina shook hands with King.

"And he's a werewolf," chirped Greg, still bouncing with excitement. Sabrina raised an eyebrow at King, who bared a couple of teeth in response.

"Long canines don't do much for me anymore, Mr. King. Got any other tricks?" She seemed unimpressed. I guessed when you hung out with vampires, battled demons, and had a cousin who was a ballet-dancing fairy you got to be a little blasé about those things.

"Yeah, but I don't think your little boyfriend here would appreciate me showing them to you."

"Unless you want to reenact *Dracula versus Wolfman* in my living room, that's probably a good choice," I said.

"So," Sabrina said. "If you two are done measuring things no one else is interested in seeing, what's the plan for the evening? Are we going after the chick who killed you and Abby, or are we rousting a bunch of frat-boy vamps at the college?"

"King wants us to split up and do both, but Greg and I said no." I pulled a chair in from the kitchen for Sabrina and looked around for a place to sit. If we kept adding supernatural associates to our little Junior Justice League, we were totally going to need a satellite. Or at least a real office.

"Why not?" Sabrina asked.

"Yeah, Jimmy, why not?" King said in a mocking sing-song.

"It's one of the first rules of horror movies, babe. Never split up."

"One of the first rules of hanging out with women who carry firearms is never call them *babe*, babe." Sabrina glared at me. "And that's dumb. We should totally split up. Abby and I will stake out the frat-vamps, while you three go deal with your sire. Or mom, or whatever you call her."

"I'm going with you?" Abigail asked, a little nervously.

"Of course, you are. We can bond. And find a twenty-four-hour Walmart and pick you up a few things. You've been wearing the same outfit for a few days now; I'm sure it's a little ripe."

"Yeah, these jeans are about ready to walk themselves to the washing machine. I'm with Cop-Girl." Abigail walked over to Greg and leaned down, putting an inordinate amount of girl-flesh in his immediate vicinity. "Greggy, can I have some cash? I need to buy a few things." My poor partner didn't even bat an eye, just walked over to his little hidey-hole under the fridge and got her a pile of cash. She threw her arms around his neck and kissed him on the cheek. I wasn't sure how he blushed on borrowed blood, but he managed.

"Ta!" she yelled over a shoulder and headed up the steps with Sabrina in tow.

I reached out and grabbed Sabrina's wrist. "Be careful," I said in a low voice. I knew Abby could hear me, but I was counting on her being distracted by the wad of cash Greg had just handed her.

"I know. She's a little flighty, but if I can keep up with you two, she should be no trouble."

"That's not what I mean. King says there are at least a dozen vamps in that house, and they've been in town for a long time. They've probably got pretty good security and, if they're any good at all, you won't know about them until it's too late. Make Abby pay attention; her senses are the only thing you've got going for you."

"Well, not the only thing. I still have my silver stake." She smiled wryly and patted a jacket pocket.

"Yeah, but only the one. Just... be careful, okay?" I leaned in even closer and whispered into her hair. "I really don't want to lose you."

She pulled back and gave me a firm look, eye to eye. "You won't." Then she kissed me, quick and fierce, before following Abigail up the stairs. I stood there for a minute thinking of the old saying, *I hate to see her go, but I love to watch her leave.*

I turned back to amused glances from Greg and King. "You got something to say?" I growled.

"Yeah," Greg said. "Where are we going to find this vampire chick?"

Chapter 11

King had tracked my sire to a new luxury hotel downtown, right next to the basketball arena. It looked like a good hunting ground, lots of out-of-towners who could be nibbled on for an hour or two without being missed. The Bobcats' season was over, but there was a concert at the arena, so the sidewalks were full of people going in and out and generally milling about. Add in the traffic to downtown watering holes, and the whole area was full of people oblivious to the predators in their midst on a mild Tuesday night. We rolled into downtown in King's truck, because he decided he wanted to be all alpha dog and drive. Plus, it appealed to the Clemson grad in me to ride around in a Silverado King Cab with the windows down and Hank Williams III blaring.

"There," King said, pulling his truck into a parking lot and pointing toward a rooftop lounge. "If I know her at all, she's up there."

"And how well do you know her, King?" My spidey-sense was going off like fireworks, but I couldn't tell if it was anything real or just nerves at seeing the vamp who had turned me after all these years. I wasn't sure whether I wanted to kill her or thank her. I supposed it was like seeing the girl from high school who dumped you right before prom, but you ended up going to prom with your future wife—except I'd never had a date to a prom, not even one that dumped me for giggles. I went to all my proms stag with Greg and Mike, and we stood against the bleachers in the gym, mocking the couples and pretending like we weren't choking on our own envy.

"I've never laid eyes on her. I've just followed the trail of bodies. Not all of them come back, you know. Some stay dead." He got a distant look in his eyes, and I didn't ask him who exactly had stayed dead to bring on this chase. Sometimes, I could be discrete. Not often, but with the full moon, life was a little crazy.

We walked into the lobby, and I had to shield my eyes against all the highly polished wood and chrome. The place looked like a piece of LA had been dropped into the middle of Charlotte, just a little too shiny for the city I knew. Greg and King made a beeline for the elevators, but I hung back, scoping out the stunning girls behind the front desk, while the boys exercised their futility for a minute or two. After standing helplessly in the elevator for a few moments, they came over to where I waited.

"You need a key to get up to the rooftop lounge," King growled.

Werewolf or not, the guy always sounded like he had something stuck in his throat.

"I figured as much. Wait here." I walked over to the front desk and almost had to cover my eyes again from the dazzling smile the woman behind the counter gave me. Her smile dropped a degree or two when she got a good look at me, but she recovered well. One downside to being turned into a vampire when you're just out of college, people in fancy hotels never took you seriously, no matter how old you really were.

"May I help you?" she asked brightly. Her nametag told me that her name was Miranda and that she was from St. Louis. That wasn't surprising. No one in Charlotte was actually from there. She had probably relocated when her dad was moved by a bank or something.

"I sure hope so, Miranda. I went out for a few drinks with the guys from the convention, and it looks like I left my key in my room. Can you run me a new one real quick?" I gave her my best harmless Southern-boy accent and waited just a second until she looked back up at me.

"Sure, can I just have your room number, Mr...?" When our eyes locked, I threw my will into my eyes and wrapped her head in my mojo.

"It doesn't matter. Just make me a key that will get me into the rooftop lounge. Then forget you ever saw me. And have a nice night." I kept my voice low and a smile on my face for the security cameras I was sure were watching.

"Yes, sir." She put a key card into the magnetic coding machine, pushed a couple of buttons, then handed it to me. "Here you go. Don't forget that you have to leave the key in the slot while you press the button for your floor." She smiled again, and I walked toward the elevators.

The boys caught up to me halfway across the lobby. King asked, "What did you do to her?"

"A little mojo." I said with a smirk. I put the key into the slot and pushed the button for the roof. As the elevator doors slid closed, I saw King's eyes narrow a little. "Don't worry," I went on. "It's harmless. And I'm pretty sure it only works on humans."

"At least it's never worked on any non-human we've ever tried it on," Greg added. "And I really don't suggest attempting to mojo a dragon."

"Yeah," I agreed. "They get testy about that stuff."

"And it's no good on zombies, either." My partner seemed determined to drag out all our failures for our newfound furry friend.

"Yeah, and demons and fairies are right out, too. Come to think of it, it doesn't even work on all humans. So you probably don't have anything to worry about," I said, needling the big guy a little.

"I'm not worried. Try that crap with me, and I'll rip out your heart and eat it. Then, I might change shape to finish you off." He gave me a frigid grin, and the elevator doors dinged open just in time.

The doors opened onto a nicely appointed rooftop terrace with several dozen well-dressed business types milling about. There was a pool with a few people swimming languidly in the underwater lights, and they were definitely the type of women who were at home wandering through a black-tie party in a bikini with no complaints. A black marble-topped bar dominated one corner of the roof, with the building to the bartender's back, and the low outer wall of the patio looked out over the skyline. I admired the lighted buildings, the arena, and the fantastical architecture of the children's theatre building just a couple blocks away.

"Where is she?" Greg asked, jostling my elbow. "Do you see her?"

I motioned for him to be quiet as I peered through the crowd, trying to find anyone familiar in the suits and party dresses. A loud group of guys wearing the oxford shirt, khaki pants, and flip-flops uniform of an off-duty bank employee cheered as they downed their tequila shots over by the ledge. As their group parted and meandered back to the bar, I saw her standing alone, watching me.

Her eyes locked with mine, and my borrowed blood ran cold when I saw a smile crawl across her lips. The smile never touched her eyes, which stayed as blue and cold as iceberg chips. She held out a hand, curling a finger in an unmistakable "come hither" gesture. I had taken a good half-dozen steps before I ran face-first into King's chest, breaking the spell and almost breaking my nose in the process. I shook my head and stepped to the side, but King put a heavy hand on my shoulder.

"I think that might be a bad idea, Junior," the werewolf said, carefully not looking straight at the vampire, who pouted beautifully at me for a second, then smiled and laughed as a man in a very expensive suit brought her a glass filled with what looked like red wine. It looked like wine at first glance, but I smelled the blood all the way across the terrace. When I looked back to where the man had come from, I saw one of the banker-boys leaning heavily on his friends, looking for all the world like a broker who'd had a little too much to drink a little too early.

"Holy crap," I whispered to Greg. "He drained that guy right here in front of everybody. And it's like nobody even noticed!" I was shocked at the new guy's actions, but even more shocked when he looked up at me and smiled a raptor smile. *He'd heard me.* With my whisper, not even a vampire should have heard me from more than a few feet away, but this guy had heard me from fifty feet. I was starting to think we might be a little out of our league.

That thought barely had time to form when the new guy smiled a little wider, showing a gleaming set of razor-sharp fangs, then whispered, "They noticed, little vampire, but they don't mind. After all, they all belong to me. These are all my people." His eyes went from emerald-green to pupil-less black in a blink, and the patio fell completely silent. I turned around slowly and saw that every single eye was focused on me and my traveling buddies, and none of them seemed happy to see us.

"Be cool," I muttered to Greg and King, who had both reached for weapons when the crowd of beautiful people suddenly turned ugly. "They're human."

"Exactly," New Guy said, who was suddenly right in front of me. I'd never even seen him start to move, and judging by the sharp intakes of breath I heard behind me, neither had the other guys. "Now, why don't we all sit down like civilized beings and discuss the impasse at which we find ourselves?"

"And what impasse would that be?" I looked anywhere but at the new vamp. If I could get brainwashed by the girl, and not by cleavage, for once, there was no telling what kind of pretzel the dude could twist my mind into.

"You would like to kill Krysta. I do not want you to. That leaves us at an impasse, wouldn't you say?" New Guy was now sitting at a table with five chairs halfway across the patio, the vamp chick beside him.

"I assume Krysta is your date's name?" I asked, showing off a little super-speed of my own by crossing the patio in the blink of an eye, then taking a seat. "I didn't catch it the last time we saw each other."

The vamp who killed me threw her head back and laughed, a silvery peal of mirth that made me want to rip her lungs out through her nose. "I had other things I was looking for that night, Mr. Black. You'll have to forgive my rudeness. I hope you've been well in the years since our last encounter. I've thought of you... often."

"Yeah, and the Easter Bunny craps jelly beans," I snarled. "You killed me and left me on my sofa! Then I woke up and murdered my best friend! All because of you!" I hadn't realized how angry I was until I looked down and saw myself standing. Greg put a hand on my shoulder and murmured appropriate noises until I took my seat.

"Well done, Mr. Knightwood. After all, discretion is the better part of valor. And we wouldn't want to ruin our lovely evening with unnecessary bloodshed, would we? Now, would anyone like a bite to eat? I find business discussions go so much better on a full stomach," New Guy said smoothly.

"Don't worry." Greg said flatly, suddenly standing right behind me. "Any bloodshed will be absolutely necessary, I promise." I glanced over at my partner and shivered a little at the look on his face. He was seriously pissed, the likes of which I hadn't seen since high school when the center for the football team used his *X-Men* collection for toilet paper. Suddenly, it looked like the werewolf was going to be the voice of reason at the party, and I had a really bad feeling about that.

"So who are you, how do you know Krysta, and why exactly shouldn't I rip out her heart and eat it?" I asked, leaning back in my chair and waving one of New Guy's human minions over. The guy came over, knelt beside my chair, and rolled up his sleeve as if it were something he did every weekend for kicks. For all I knew, it was. With bravado I didn't feel, I sank my teeth into his wrist and took a big drink, my eyes never leaving Krysta. She smiled a slow smile as she watched me drink, and the hair on the back of my neck went up again. Something about this whole scene wasn't right, and New Guy's next words told me how unfortunately correct I was.

Chapter 12

"My name is Gordon Tiram, and this is my city." New Guy looked over the patio like a feudal lord, which I supposed he had just declared himself. I dropped the arm of the human I was munching on and gaped up at the vampire who had just declared himself my new boss.

"What do you mean, *your* city?" Greg sneered, despite my trying to wave him to silence. Usually running off at the mouth was my shtick, but apparently Greg had appointed himself Dumb Question Guy for the evening. I was starting to see just how annoying it could be to an observer.

"I mean, Mr. Knightwood, that I am the Master of Charlotte. All vampiric activity within the metropolitan area falls under my dominion. Krysta here has paid appropriate tribute as a visitor to my territory, and I have given her my protection. That extends to all my subjects, including yourself and Mr. Black. So you will not harm her without my permission, which I will not give. Do I make myself clear?"

Greg started to answer, and I gave up on trying to subtly shush him. Instead, I reached over and punched him in the gut. He let out an "oof!" and shot me a nasty look, but I ignored it and started talking fast and thinking faster. If I didn't come up with something pretty quick, we were going to end up in a big fight with two seriously powerful vampires and a couple dozen humans. I wasn't at all sure we could win, and I knew we couldn't win without making a lot of well-dressed corpses.

"So," I began. "Is Master of the City a city-only position, or is it like most things around here, a city-county collective? I mean, are you the Master of Charlotte, or are you the Charlotte-Mecklenburg Master of the City? I just wanna know if I have to ask permission just within the city limits, or does your control reach all the suburbs, too? And what about neighboring counties? Are you more like the Master of the Greater Charlotte Viewing Area, because I don't watch much TV, and that might be tough. And did we enlist in your little army, or were we drafted? Because our mail service has been really spotty for the last fifteen years or so, and I think I might have eaten the guy who brought me the certified letter telling me that I work for you." I paused to take a breath and check for reactions, but Tiram just sat there smiling what he probably considered an enigmatic smile. I guessed it was, since I had no idea what it meant, but I wasn't about to admit to that.

"I have heard of your legendary wit, Mr. Black. Now I see that those reports are at best half-true." I put on my best wounded expression, but he went on, "I am the Master of the City, and my territory extends to all vampires living, if you'll pardon the term, within the region. There is another Master in Atlanta, and a different one in Washington. But you only need concern yourself with me. And you do need to be concerned with me, Mr. Black. Because you are correct, you cannot defeat me. You cannot even hope to survive a moment of my displeasure. So please, sit." He laid a lot of mojo on the last word, and my butt was in the chair before the sound died on his lips.

"Now," he said. "I understand that you feel you have an unresolved disagreement with Krysta, and that Mr. King here has convinced you she is an evil creature, murdering willy-nilly all across the country. But I assure you that she is not, and that Mr. King here is mistaken. And you gentlemen would like nothing better than to forget all about this unpleasant encounter and go back to your ridiculously boring existence." I felt the weight of his words, and he made a lot of sense. I mean, why would a vampire like Krysta, obviously someone of good breeding, run around killing random people? It just didn't make sense.

I was halfway out of my chair when Greg spoke up. "Are you done playing Boggle with his brain yet? Because it's not working on me or Jo-Jo the Dog-Faced Boy, and I really hate to see Jimmy so confused all the time." I shook my head to clear it and realized that Tiram had put the mojo on me something fierce. Greg and King were apparently immune to the effects, but I'd bought it—hook, line, and sinker. I was totally going to have to take up yoga or some of that other meditation crap Sabrina kept yammering about.

"Interesting. My words had no effect on you at all?" Tiram asked Greg.

"Yeah, they annoyed me. You're a pompous ass, and your girlfriend is a mass murderer. And we're going to kill her. Now how many of your walking hors d'oeuvres are you willing to sacrifice to protect her?" Greg got to his feet, a samurai sword coming from somewhere to end up in one hand, and a pistol in his other. I took a second to look, but I couldn't figure out where he'd kept that sword hidden—must have been uncomfortable, wherever it was.

"Fascinating. Your mind is so much stronger than your friend's," the Master of the City mused.

"That sets the bar pretty low, pal. Now, can we get back to the question at hand? Namely, are you going to get out of the way so we can off your arm ornament, or is this going to get ugly?" Greg was pretty intense, and King looked as if he were ready for a fight, but I was still having a hard time clearing my head.

Everything got very clear very quickly when Krysta reached out and grabbed a pretty waitress by the throat. "Put away the sword, fat boy. I'll happily kill this human and leave the mess for you to deal with." She held out her other hand, clawlike, and I could see her ripping the girl's throat in my mind.

"Okay, kids, let's everybody calm down." I stepped forward with both hands out, trying to defuse the situation a little. "Nobody wants to hurt anybody here; we just want to talk."

"Actually, Mr. Black, I'm pretty sure we all want to kill each other," Tiram said, his eyes never leaving my partner.

"I know that. I just didn't have anything better to say, and I needed to get a little closer."

"Closer?" he parroted.

"Yeah, so I could do this." I drew my Glock and shot Krysta in the wrist, shattering both bones in her forearm and causing her to drop the waitress.

I grabbed the human girl before she hit the floor and looked her in the eyes. "Run," I said, my voice low and heavy with mojo. "Get out of here and don't stop running until you're at least three blocks away."

She took off as if the hounds of hell were on her heels and, when I turned around, I thought she might have been right. King had obviously taken my hint to get ready for a fight, because where a tall guy with a monobrow had stood seconds before, there was now a seven-foot-tall wolf-man with claws like razorblades and a seriously grumpy look on his face. Or muzzle. Or whatever you call it.

Greg and I got shoulder to shoulder with the wolf-man and squared off to face the other vampires, but Tiram hadn't moved. "Do you three really think you can defeat us?" he asked with a cold smile.

"Not really," I answered honestly. "But I think we can take one of you. And I bet neither one of you selfish chumps wants to be the one we take." I leveled my pistol at Krysta's face, and Greg lined up his sword on Tiram. King growled low in his throat and bunched his muscles to leap into the fray.

Chapter 13

Just as our pet wolf-man was about to pounce, I felt a huge impact on the side of my head and was knocked to the patio. I broke my fall with my hands, but my gun went skittering across the concrete and right into the swimming pool. Contrary to popular fiction, a good pistol will fire even when wet, but I hated swimming, and I was wearing my favorite pants. I had just about enough time to realize all of this before I felt a rush of air toward my head. I rolled over in time to see a spiked heel slam down right where my temple had been half a second before. I looked up to see a beautiful human woman in a very short skirt trying to stomp me to death. I had no real time to enjoy the view because she quickly lined up for a second stab with her stiletto heels. I clambered to my feet with all the grace a scrawny vampire could muster, which wasn't much, and caught her fist as it flew toward my eye.

"Sleep," I said as we locked eyes. Nothing. I heard Tiram chuckle behind me and chanced a glance over my shoulder. He was leaning against the bar sipping a drink with an umbrella and smirking at me while the babe in the miniskirt landed a solid punch on my cheek. *All right,* I thought, *the hard way it is.* I took the shot to the face while still holding her other hand and, as she drew back again, I reached out and slapped her to the ground. I felt bad about it for about half a second but, when she kicked up and caught me in the shin with a heel, all remorse went out the window. I ducked under a punch thrown by another blank-eyed yuppie in party clothes and picked up the first chick by the collar and one leg. I lifted her easily over my head and threw her into the pool, taking out a waiter and a tray of drinks in the process.

I looked around, and Greg and King were similarly occupied with mesmerized bankers and their tarted-up girls *du jour*. One guy jumped on King's fuzzy back and beat him in the head with a Blackberry, while Greg used his sword to deflect glassware hurled at him by two women near the bar. Another mortal rushed at me, head down and feet churning until all I needed to complete the picture was a red cape and some tight pants. I dodged, picked him up by the scruff of the neck and his belt as he passed, and pitched him into the pool on top of the first girl, who was just climbing out.

King flipped the guy off his back, and I looked on in horror as he wrapped a huge furry fist around the human's throat. He leaned in, fangs bared and eyes narrowed, and drew back his other hand for the killing stroke. Just before he ripped the man's face off, Greg ducked under a flying highball glass, which then caught King a solid blow to the temple. His yellow eyes rolled back in his head, and the giant wolf-man collapsed on top of the human he'd been about to eviscerate.

"Nice timing!" I yelled to Greg.

"Thanks!" he shouted back. "You got any bright ideas?"

"Yeah, don't kill the humans!"

"Got it!" He shattered two martini glasses with a swipe of his sword.

I heard the squeak of a leather shoe behind me and ducked under a punch that would have knocked me into the middle of next week. I looked up, and up, and up, into the largest human I'd ever seen up close. Almost seven feet tall and wider than most doorways, he stood over me like a very grumpy bald mountain with a goatee and more tattoos than the entire lineup of Mötley Crüe. He drew back a fist that looked bigger than Rhode Island and swung for my head. Fortunately, he was almost as slow as I'd hoped, and I ducked his punch easily. Unfortunately, he wasn't as stupid as I'd hoped and, by ducking under his haymaker, I put my face right in front of the uppercut he threw behind it. It felt like a lead-lined Christmas ham hit me right on the point of my jaw, and I flew a good five feet before crashing into a glass and metal patio table. Steel bent, glass shattered, and one undernourished vampire got wrapped up in lawn furniture like a grievously wounded pretzel.

The walking mountain came at me again. I tried to stand, but I was too tangled in table parts. He helped me to my feet, if by *helped* one could refer to picking me up, table and all, over his head, and throwing me twenty feet into the swimming pool. I sank to the bottom instantly and would have drowned in seconds except for one little advantage I had going for me: I breathed out of habit, not necessity. Drowning was still uncomfortable, but it wouldn't kill me. As I got nothing from air, holding my breath indefinitely wasn't a real issue, so I felt a little like Br'er Rabbit in the middle of the briar patch down where it was cooler and no one was trying to crush my head. I took a few seconds to disengage from the mangled table and looked around for my pistol while I was down there. No luck. I figured it had been sucked into a vent or something. I made my way as stealthily as possible to a ladder and climbed out of the pool on the side away from the fracas.

Greg seemed to be holding his own, swatting glassware out of the air like Luke Skywalker in Lightsaber 101. Every once in a while, one of the minions would get brave and dart in for a punch, but Greg always smacked them back with the flat of his blade. I was actually impressed, which might explain how I missed the dripping wet minx in the miniskirt aiming my gun at my best friend's back and pulling the trigger half a dozen times. Before I could react, Greg was down with a tight grouping of new orifices in his back, and the mesmerized woman had turned the gun in my direction. There was most of a patio and a swimming pool separating us, but I covered the entire distance in one very pissed-off leap. I landed in front of her and knocked the gun out of her hand before she got off a round. I punched her in the jaw and had the small satisfaction of seeing her eyes roll back into her head as she collapsed to the deck.

The noise of the gunshots had shaken the mojo out of some of the revelers, and they were looking around in bewilderment. Then one guy looked down at Greg, saw the bullet holes, and screamed like a seventh-grade girl at a Justin Bieber concert. That sparked a stampede for the elevators, and I found myself swimming upstream trying to get to my partner's side. I finally reached him, but about two seconds too late. Krysta had Greg by the throat, and I was even more impressed by her strength when she casually lifted his bulk into the air with one hand. She was a tall woman, so getting him off the ground wasn't an issue, but Greg had never been what anyone would call svelte. She smiled at me, then looked over at King, who was just now regaining consciousness, albeit in human form.

"Now, little vampire," Krysta said, with a smile that made my blood run cold. Or maybe that was just from my dip in the pool. Either way, it was getting chilly. "Whatever shall I do with this sack of meat? He's no good for a plaything; he's much too homely. You were bad enough, but I took pity on you and shared of myself. But this?" She gave Greg's limp body a shake. "This thing isn't even worth keeping around." Once finished insulting my manhood and my friend, she casually tossed my partner over the side of the patio to the sidewalk some sixteen stories below. I ran to the edge and looked over, seeing just the last second of his fall before Greg hit the unforgiving concrete with a wet thwack.

I spun around, my vision completely red, but Krysta and Tiram were nowhere to be seen. I was alone on a patio with a half-dressed, semi-conscious werewolf, five comatose partygoers, who had been subdued during the fight, and one very nervous security guard, who had just gotten off the elevator. I threw King over my shoulder, nodded to the guard, and got in the elevator.

I pushed the "L" button, while the guard stared at me, dismayed.

"Lightweight," I said, nodding to King's incoherent, and very heavy, carcass. Then, the doors slid shut, and I went down to try and scrape my partner off the sidewalk before the cops showed up.

Chapter 14

Through a combination of insults and slaps to the head, I managed to get King ambulatory by the time we reached the lobby. We walked quickly toward the doors, ignoring the frightened looks we got from the humans as we headed for the front door. A crowd had started to gather around Greg's inert form by the time I got there, and I had to push my way to his side. It was tough going for the first few feet, then they noticed I had a giant wolf-guy in tow, and the crowd parted like grease in a Dawn commercial. I knelt by Greg's side and pretended to feel for a pulse, while I tried to inconspicuously shake him awake.

"Play dead," I whispered.

"I am dead," I heard him mutter back. A huge weight lifted off my shoulders when I realized that defenestration had been moved onto "Will Not Kill Vampires" list, and I went ahead with my plan. I reached down and grabbed one arm, pulling him carelessly to his feet.

"Hey, watch out!" I heard somebody yell from the crowd. A few other onlookers shouted concern for his wellbeing, and I turned to address the crowd.

"What? Don't you people read the paper? This is a stunt dummy. We're shooting outtakes for the new Will Smith movie. The cameras are in the van over there." I pointed at a parking lot across the street. "This isn't even a person. Here, feel the skin. Cold as the grave, right?" I held Greg's arm out to the nearest old lady, and she shrieked appropriately. I hefted Greg into a fireman's carry across my shoulders and started making my slow way to the car. The crowd, disappointed that no one had died, parted, but not without three guys slipping me business cards and telling me they were stuntmen or extras. I thought about telling them King was really Vin Diesel, but decided we didn't need autograph seekers.

King backed his truck out of its parking space, and I tossed Greg into the back, hopping in beside him. King pulled onto the street, his tires barking and laying a stinking strip of rubber behind us. Greg let out a feeble groan when we hit a set of railroad tracks, and I grabbed his head to hold it steady. I wasn't sure if he'd broken his neck, or if even we could live through that, but the last thing I wanted was for him to end up paralyzed. Visions of being caregiver to an immortal quadriplegic vampire flashed through my head, and none of them were pleasant.

I banged on the cab. "Slow down! I am not spoon-feeding this vegetable for the next six hundred years!" King looked back with a puzzled expression, but slowed as we headed out of town toward our cemetery. I pulled out my pocketknife and opened up my wrist. I held Greg's head higher and pressed my wrist to his mouth so he could regain a little strength.

He latched on to my arm like a drowning man grabbing for a rubber ducky, and I felt the blood flow from my wrist into his mouth. I let him feed for a minute or two before I felt my strength start to ebb, then I pried him off. He'd gotten a bit of color back and was able to sit up a little.

"You okay?" I asked.

"Now I know how that coyote felt in the cartoons."

"I would hit you for that, but I'm afraid it might kill you."

"Yeah, me, too." He closed his eyes and leaned back against the cab of the truck. "I thought I was done for, man. I thought she was going to break my neck right there. I haven't been that scared in a long time." He kept his eyes closed, but even in the flickering streetlights I saw a hint of moisture around the lids.

I put a hand on his shoulder. "Me, too, bro. Me, too. I'm just glad you've got a little bounce to you. I'd hate to train a new partner after all these years."

"Yeah, like you could find anybody else who'd put up with you." He chuckled lightly, and I felt him pull back from the edge a little. Greg's always taken things a lot harder than me. Even back in middle school when the jocks shoved us in lockers and flew our underwear up the flagpole, he took it to heart. Me, I just shrugged it off and put sugar in their gas tanks.

We got clear of downtown, and I banged on the cab again to get King to pull over. He pulled into a fast food restaurant parking lot and got out of the truck. "Look, bloodsucker, if you dent my cab, there's gonna be hell to pay." He'd shifted back into human form, but apparently whatever magic made him change didn't make his clothes change, too. The only things that had survived the shift were his boxer briefs, and it looked like he'd stretched some of the elastic to the limit, judging by how he held them up with one hand. I smirked a little, and he reached behind the seat for a suitcase.

"Congratulations, King, you really are a redneck." I complimented the baffled werewolf as he unpacked a Lynyrd Skynyrd t-shirt and a tattered pair of jeans.

"He went to Clemson. He knows a redneck when he sees one," Greg affirmed.

"Good, you're not dead," King said to my battered partner.

"Well, technically…" I started, but gave up. "I need to get something to eat. Wait here." I started walking, but stopped short when I realized King was following me.

"What are you doing?" I asked.

"I'm hungry, too. I burned a lot of calories shifting, and getting the crap knocked out of me didn't help."

"Really?" I looked at him incredulously. "You don't think I'm going to get a burger and fries, do you? Hello? Vampire? Remember, undead creature of the night? Now piss off for a few minutes while I reload the tank, and then you can go get a Happy Meal." I stalked off to the kitchen entrance, turning as I got to the door to see King in the middle of the parking lot staring after me like a very confused dog, the one who finally caught a car and now has no idea what to do with it. Yeah, that was the look.

I took a position beside the kitchen door and only had to wait about five minutes before a grumpy Latino kid came out for a smoke break. He tapped a cigarette out of a pack from his shirt pocket, and then almost jumped out of his Reeboks as I spoke up behind him. "You know that stuff'll stunt your growth."

"*Dios mio!* What the hell are you doing there, man? You trying to scare somebody to death?" The kid picked his lit cigarette up off the ground and looked up at me. Our eyes locked, and I pushed my will into his head, taking him over in the blink of an eye.

"Stand up." He did. "When this is over, you will remember nothing. You went out for a smoke, it wasn't very good, and you decided to quit. You will never smoke again. You'll finish school and go to college. You will study hard and work hard and make a good career for yourself." I tried to lay as much positive reinforcement on him as possible in the few seconds I had, then I grabbed the kid by the shirt and pulled him close to me. I bent his head to the side and bit deep into his neck. I felt his blood against the back of my throat like a hot crimson fountain. I could almost taste his heartbeat through the rush of blood into my mouth. My body gulped it down, starving to replace what I'd given Greg and what I'd burned up in the fight. The kid moaned a little as I drank, and I heard my own throat echo him. He sagged, and I put my other arm around his back to support him. I drank deeper than I'd intended and felt his heart falter a touch before I gave myself a mental shake and pulled back from him. I held him gently as he collapsed to the ground, then I leaned him up against the wall in a seated position. I ran a finger over his throat and used the tail of my t-shirt to wipe away the blood seeping from the already closed wounds.

75

I stood up, a little dizzy from the influx of new blood and the nicotine in the kid's system, and made my wobbly way back to the truck. King was sitting on the tailgate eating a sack full of cheeseburgers, and Greg shot me a disappointed look as I hopped into the bed of the truck. I said nothing, just reached over and took a long slurp of King's super-sized coke. "Too much cola's bad for you," I said by way of explanation as he snatched his drink away from me.

"Yeah, and drinking my cola's bad for *you*," he snarled, setting the drink well out of my reach. He wiped at the straw where I'd left a little red stain behind and looked at me quizzically.

"You don't want to know," I said.

"Then I already know."

"Then you don't need to ask, so same difference. We can go whenever you're ready."

"And where are we going, exactly?" King asked, finishing off the last of what looked like a dozen cheeseburgers. He walked a few feet to throw the bag in a nearby garbage can.

"Home. We need to plan some more before we go back after Krysta and her boyfriend. And Greg needs a place to heal up. And I could use a beer. Or seven."

"Sounds good enough. Let's roll." King hopped back behind the wheel, and Greg grabbed shotgun. I was stuck in the backseat trying to find a comfortable place to put my feet among weeks' worth of fast food wrappers, soda bottles, and dirty clothes. And I thought Greg and I kept a messy house.

Chapter 15

All thoughts of our housekeeping skills went out the window the second we pulled into the cemetery, because it was pretty obvious we wouldn't be keeping house there anymore. A pillar of black smoke reached for the sky, and flames leaped a good twenty feet into the air as we parked in front of what used to be our caretaker's cottage and underground lair. I jumped out of the truck and ran toward the house, but King grabbed me before I covered any real ground.

"It's gone, man." He held me off the ground, feet churning like a cartoon character. "There's nothing in there that survived." I relaxed in his arms with the realization that he was right; everything we owned was gone.

Just as I was starting to mourn the loss of my comic collection, I heard a girl's voice rising above the flames in a tortured scream.

"Abby!" I yelled, twisting free of King's grasp and falling to the turf. My hands and feet clawed the ground uselessly for a couple of precious seconds as I tried frantically to get everything working together. Finally, I heaved myself off the grass and bolted into the burning house, yelling for Abby the whole way.

For the second time in one night, it was very handy that I didn't have to breathe, because the smoke poured from our underground apartment in thick black tendrils. I leaped down the stairs, crashing through the last few and gashing open my left leg. I fell face-first with my hands in a puddle of blue-tinged flame, then hastily beat out my burning sleeves as I fought to disengage from the splintered wood. I took a quick look around at an apartment fully engulfed in fire. Our furniture had been piled together in the center of the den to make a pyre, and something had obviously been poured around the whole room to make it burn like that. I pulled myself loose from the steps with a sick sound of tearing flesh, and yelled again for Abby. I doubled over coughing as I drew in smoky air to shout again, but I was able to get low enough to see her feet dangling from the far wall.

I got down on my hands and knees and pulled open the door to the coat closet at the bottom of the stairs. I yanked my leather duster off a hanger and covered my head and shoulders with it. I blew out as much foul smoke as I could get from my scalded lungs and commando-crawled across the floor to where I had seen Abby's feet. I got to her with vamp speed, but lost a few precious seconds trying to figure out how she was floating on the wall. By the time I got to my feet, the fire had surrounded us, and I had no clear path back to the stairs.

I turned back to Abby, and it finally sunk in why she was still in the apartment with all that fire—she'd been nailed to the wall and couldn't pull herself free. Thick silver stakes pierced her forearms just behind the wrist, then had been driven into the wall, holding her a good foot off the ground. Abby moaned and tried to pull away when I shook her shoulder to bring her around. I grabbed one of the stakes and tried to pull it from the wall, but it only wiggled between the bones of her arm, making her scream in agony. I yelled a little too because the hot silver burned my hand, then yelled again when I noticed the back of my duster coated with flames. I ripped off the coat and beat out the fire in a semicircle a few feet around us, then reached back up to grab the stake again.

"Abby," I said, trying to get her attention on my face instead of the pain in her arm. "We're gonna do this on three, okay?" She nodded weakly, and I started to count. "One, two," and on "two," I yanked with every ounce of strength in me. The stake came free, and Abby sagged onto me, howling. She screamed and thrashed around, clawing my arm and shoulder to ribbons where I tried to hold her up and beat back the fire at the same time. I reached over and yanked her other arm free, but this time the spike stayed stuck in her arm, and they both came free from the wall. *I'll take what I can get,* I thought as I turned back to where my stairs used to be.

There was nothing there, just a pillar of fire reaching out into the cemetery. Abby was thrashing and fighting like a crazed animal, so I set her down on her feet. She whirled on me and went for my throat, fangs out, but I was ready. I put one wrist in her mouth, effectively blocking her mouth open, then punched her in the side of the head with enough force to crush a human's skull like an egg. Fortunately, vampires don't get concussions and, with her stake wounds and burns, I didn't think she'd even notice when she woke up. I tossed her over my shoulder and decided if I was going to carry them all the time, I had to get skinnier friends.

I stomped out the last shreds of my duster and covered Abby's face with it, then ran and jumped my way across the minefield my apartment had become. I reached the hole under where the stairs used to be and gathered all my strength for a vertical leap. I heard the crackling sounds of walls collapsing above and jumped for all I was

worth for clean air and sky. I hurtled up through the fire like a
scrawny, retarded phoenix, landing just long enough for my pants to
catch fire, then I executed another jump that would have made Jordan
retire out of pure jealousy. With solid ground under me, I hotfooted—
pun intended—it back to the truck where Greg and King were
waiting. King pulled a small fire extinguisher from his rolling garbage
dump of a vehicle and sprayed us down.

I dumped Abby into the bed of the truck and hopped in beside
her. "Get us the hell out of here," I yelled, then fell to my knees as
King floored the gas pedal. I had just enough time to make it to the
side of the truck before the contents of my stomach and lungs came
up. Black bits of ash mixed with blood and beer as King shifted into
high gear and booked it out of the cemetery just as the emergency
vehicles started rolling in. I reached into my pocket for my phone to
text Sabrina. Then, suddenly, the really bad news hit me. Despite the
fact that my shoes were still smoldering, I got goosebumps and
started to shake uncontrollably.

"What's wrong with you?" King asked through the rear window
of the truck.

"Sabrina wasn't in there."

"That's good, right?"

"No," Greg said from the passenger seat.

"They've got her," I clarified, staring at the lightening horizon.

"Are you sure?" King asked.

"She wasn't in the house. I would have smelled her. They took
Sabrina," I said. "And it's almost sunrise."

"So you can't go after them," he replied.

"And I'm not even sure who *them* is."

"Of course we're sure! We know exactly who has her. Her and
Barbie back there went to look in on your vamp-frat. That's gotta be
who did this."

"We think, but for all we know it was more of the Master's
minions while we were tangling with Krysta."

"That sound right to you?"

"No."

"Me, neither. So, where to?"

"Only one place we can go when all hope is lost." I pointed him
toward a left turn.

"A bar?"

"Church."

Chapter 16

The sky was getting light when we pulled into St. Patrick's. I directed King around to the rectory. I beat on the door for what felt like an hour until a sleepy young priest finally opened it.

"Can I help you?" he mumbled, tugging his shirt around to get the collar just right.

"Where's Mike?" I demanded.

"I'm sorry, sir. Father Mike is on medical leave for a few weeks. He's having surgery today." *Oh, crap.* I'd forgotten about Mike's surgery in all the fighting, shooting, and burning. "Is there something I can help you with?"

"No, thanks, Father. It's personal with Mike and me. We go way back." I saw the humor in his eyes and remembered that I had stopped aging at twenty-three. Mike and I were the same age, but he looked a lot older than his almost-forty, while I still got carded from time to time when buying booze. Good thing for me I usually stole my booze from my dinner dates.

The young priest asked again if I needed any help and, while help was exactly what I needed, or at least near the top of the list, I couldn't ask for help or blood from an unsuspecting clergyman. I thanked him again and limped back to the truck. My back and neck were really starting to sting from the fire, and I just hoped that I could heal burns, or Abby and I weren't going to be nearly so attractive anymore. Greater loss for her than for me, but I'd grown accustomed to my face, as the song went, and I didn't want it to be all melty for the rest of eternity.

"What's wrong?" King asked, as I got back in the truck.

"My contact at the church, who happens to be one of my very best friends in the world, is in the hospital having a tumor the size of a golf ball removed from his esophagus today. I'd completely forgotten about this relatively important event because my house was just burned down. Or up, since it was a basement. My best friend and business partner is in the back of a werewolf's pickup truck trying to heal from being thrown off a roof, and my new protégé is sharing the bed of said pickup with him while she tries not to scream in agony from being staked to a wall and set on fire. Add the fact that I just got my ass kicked by the Master of the City, a vampire I never even knew existed, and I'm having a pretty crappy night. Oh, yeah, and the closest thing I've had to a girlfriend since 1993 was just kidnapped by a group of stoner vampires, and I can't do anything about it because the sun is coming up. So as far as 'what's wrong' goes, did I leave anything out?" My voice might have gotten a little shrill by the end of my recitation, and the possibility existed that I bared a little more fang than I really intended, but those things could happen.

"Nah, I think you covered it," King replied. "So what are you gonna do about it?"

"Thanks to this little issue I have with the sun, which is quickly rising, I'm going to do the only thing I can—namely, hide until it's dark again."

"Sounds like a fair plan."

"I'm so glad you approve. Now, do you have anywhere we can crash, preferably with a supply of B-Negative in the fridge?"

"Nope, my hotel is probably under surveillance, and it has too many windows, anyway."

"All righty then, Plan D it is." I opened the door and dropped the tailgate.

"Plan D?" The werewolf asked, as I tossed Abby over my shoulder and started walking into the cemetery behind the church.

"Yeah, grab Greg and follow me," I called over my shoulder.

"Follow you where?" he asked, but he did as I said.

Where was a sizable crypt Greg and I had used on a few occasions when we were having issues with hallowed ground. It turned out that was all a psychological thing, not a mystical thing, but it never hurt to have a few extra hideouts up your sleeve. Or in your armpits if your sleeves had been burned off. The crypt was one of those old family ones that were more common in New Orleans than North Carolina, and there were no dates more recent than 1910, so we'd used it from time to time to crash. There was a big open space in the middle, a couple of benches on one wall, and about two dozen plaques on another wall where the coffins were stored. I dropped Abby onto one of the benches, and King settled Greg on the floor along the wall with the plaques.

When we had the wounded settled as comfortably as possible, I sagged against the wall furthest from the door. King sat with his back blocking the door, just in case anyone got too enterprising during the day, and we tried to get a few hours rest before I went off to tear a pack of vampires into little bat-shaped pieces.

That whole thing about us passing out as soon as the sun came up was a myth, like so much of what people had written about us over the years but, the second I sat down, the events of the night caught up with me, and all the anger, fear, and pain washed over me like a tidal wave. I went crashing down into a deep sleep for the next eight hours or so.

I woke up with a stiff neck and a bad attitude. Greg and Abby were still out of it, both looking terrible. King's eyes snapped open the second I stirred and, by the time I had my feet under me, he was standing with a hand under his jacket. "Relax," I said. "Nothing going on, just me." The werewolf relaxed and sat back down against the door. I paced the crypt for the next few hours until Greg started to stir.

"Where are we?" he asked, rubbing his head and wincing at the new bruises he'd accumulated in his fall.

"Crypt behind Mike's place," I muttered.

"Why aren't we inside? You know, where the beds are?" Greg stood and tried to stretch the kinks out of his back, but he was still too beat up to stand for more than a few seconds.

"Mike's in the hospital. His surgery was this morning."

"Crap. I forgot."

"Yeah, me, too. Your phone still work?" I asked, holding out my hand.

"If I didn't land on it." He dug around in his utility belt. "Here you go. What happened to yours?" he asked, tossing me his phone.

I dialed Sabrina's cousin from memory. "I went swimming, remember? Stephen? Is that you? Good. It's Jimmy. I don't have time to explain, but I need a favor." We'd helped Stephen out of a bit of trouble a few months ago and given him a break on the fee, so I knew he'd help. "Can you go to the hospital? Our friend Mike had surgery this morning, and it would mean a lot to me if you would go check on him. Yeah, just call me back at this number and lemme know how he's doing. Sabrina? She's fine. I think she's working right now. No, I haven't talked to her today. I was sleeping most of the day. Yeah, when I see her I'll tell her." I pushed the button to end the call and caught Greg's look.

"Yeah," I said. "They kidnapped Sabrina and almost roasted Abby last night while you and I were out playing Batman."

"I wondered why Abby smelled singed," Greg said. "Where did they take her?"

"I don't know. They didn't exactly leave a note." I sat back down against a wall.

"But they sure sent a message, didn't they?" King said from his spot by the door.

"What's that mean?" Greg asked.

"Yeah, about that…" I hesitated.

"What?" Greg demanded.

"We're kinda homeless." I waited for the explosion.

"How can you be *kinda* homeless? Isn't that like *kinda* pregnant?" My partner would have been red-faced by this point if he'd had enough blood in him to flow.

"Okay, good point," I admitted. "We're homeless. The college vamps burned our place down. Or up, if you consider the fact that we lived in a hole in the ground."

"Burned?" Greg asked in a small voice. I watched him processing the things lost in the fire—his video games, his computers, comic book collection, probably some exotic porn that I didn't really want to think about.

"Yeah, burned. And they tried pretty hard to kill Abby in the process."

"And let me tell you, I'm pissed about that," Abby said in a weak voice. "Now is there anybody to drink in this…where are we?" She tried to stand and failed, so she slumped back down next to Greg on the wall opposite me.

"Sorry, kiddo. All my reserves went to Captain Sidewalk Pizza over there last night. I got nothing left. And as to where, we're in a crypt behind a church."

"Here, take a little. But let go when I tell you to, or I'll break your fangs off." King knelt in front of Abby and Greg with his sleeves rolled up. Abby locked onto the proffered arm with gusto, but Greg held back.

"C'mon, bro, you gotta eat something or you won't even be able to walk, much less help me find Sabrina," I cajoled.

"Just drink, kid. It's the full moon, so I heal even faster than usual. I'll be back to normal in a couple of hours, even if you two were to drain me almost dry. And I ain't letting that happen." King stuck his arm back under Greg's nose. My vegan partner stared at it for a few seconds, then the pain of his wounds and his hunger won out, and he bit into the werewolf's arm and started to drink. I sat against the wall, mouth watering, while my partner and our protégé drank enough from King to heal most of their wounds. It only took a few minutes before he shook them off his wrists and pulled a dirty bandana out of his back pocket.

I went over to him, tore the rag in half, and bound the wounds. "You know they'll heal almost instantly, right?"

"Yeah, but those two are still pretty hungry, and I'd like to keep any blood covered while they get their wits about them."

"You're pretty smart for a Labrador." I tied off the last knot and ducked as he took a swing at me.

"Thanks. And you're not half-bad for a soulless bloodsucking parasite."

"One does what one can. How are they?" I asked, looking over at my partner.

"I'm fine," Greg answered irritably, swatting my hand aside when I tried to check his pupils.

"You must be fine if you're grumpy." I went over to Abigail. She still looked pretty rough, and she sat with her back to the crypt, none of her normal attitude in evidence. "How about you?" I asked.

"I'm okay," she said in a blank voice that told me she was anything but. She sat staring at nothing, rubbing her wrists where the stakes had been driven through.

"It's understandable if you're scared. They really did a number on you. I don't—"

She cut me off with a look. Her eyes were cold, almost completely soulless. The only thing they reminded me of was the way the Master of the City had looked—completely predatory.

"I'm fine. They're the ones you should be worried about. When do we leave?" She stood up, but wobbled a bit, still unsteady on her feet.

"*We* aren't going anywhere. You two are staying here with the furry bloodbank, at least for tonight." I held up my hand at their protests. "Come on. You both know you're too weak, and it's the peak of the full moon, so I can't take Fluffy here with me anywhere. You guys might as well stay here, take the occasional nibble from the regenerating fountain of youth, and let me do what I do."

"And what is it that you do, exactly?" a dizzy King grumbled from his spot on the floor.

"I hit things and make huge messes."

I headed out to do just that.

Chapter 17

I wasn't really angry when I left the crypt. The last rays of sunlight made me squint and gave my skin that nice rosy tint that either said, "vampire got out of bed too early," or "ginger kid stayed at the beach too long." It was more a cold feeling in the pit of my stomach, that feeling a person got when they knew they were going to do a large number of very bad things to people before the night's work was finished.

It wasn't a good feeling, but that was where I was when I got into King's Silverado and headed down to Wilkinson Boulevard. Wilkinson was home to all the porn stores, strip clubs, and pawnshops one could ask for, with a gigantic country bar thrown in for good measure. Since I wasn't in the mood for line dancing, my internal compass led me straight to the biggest pawnshop in town. I walked in just as the owner was trying to lock the front door.

"Sorry, man. We closed. You gotta come back tomorrow." He was six foot six and three hundred pounds of large black dude with no hair and enough gold around his neck to give Mr. T a chubby. He put his hand on my chest and tried to push me back toward the door. That didn't go so well for him. I broke his arm below the elbow, so he'd only have to wear the short cast, but that was the only consideration I gave him. He was tough, though; he went for his gun with his left hand. I picked him up by his belt and held him over my head for a few seconds, just staring at him. I couldn't get my head on straight enough to mojo him but, apparently, being hoisted into the air by a skinny white kid with fangs made him decide discretion was the better part of valor. He dropped the gun, and I set him down.

"I don't want no trouble, man. Lemme go, and you can have whatever you want." He sank to his knees in front of me, and big tears started to roll down his round face.

"Open the safe."

"I don't got the combination, man. You gots to believe me." He was really crying at this point, but his eyes kept flicking behind me to the door, as if expecting somebody. I heard soft footsteps and the sound of somebody trying very quietly to cock a revolver, and I was on the move.

I jumped one of the shelves with an easy hop and ran around behind my new attacker. A kid, barely sixteen, stood in the aisle looking very confused and holding a .38. I tapped him on the shoulder, and said "Boo," when he turned around. The kid jumped and yelled a little, and the gun went off, the bullet ricocheting off the floor into a shelf. I quickly snatched the gun from him and slapped him across the face.

"That's why children shouldn't play with guns. Now get out of here." He looked in my eyes for about half a second before he decided to take my advice. He ran like hell itself was behind him, and I turned my attention back to the sobbing mountain of humanity in the floor.

"Open. The. Safe." I leaned in, showing my fangs, and the fat guy nodded. He went around behind the counter and, when he knelt down to open the safe, I continued, "If you do anything with the gun in there except hand it over quietly, I'll eat your spleen and make you watch." I don't even really know what a spleen looked like, or where it was in the body, but it sounded good. Tiny pulled a couple of stacks of cash out of the safe, along with a Glock 19.

"I'm gonna go out on a limb here and guess that gun mysteriously doesn't have any serial numbers on it," I mused quietly.

"I don't know nothing about that, man. I just work here. You broke the shit out of my arm. Why you gotta do that?"

"Seemed like a good idea at the time. Now, do you want to open the gun cases, or should I break the glass?"

"I guess I'll get in less trouble with the boss if you break the glass, so go ahead." So I did. I broke into the display cases and loaded up with another pair of Glocks, half a dozen magazines, and three boxes of ammunition. A short-barreled pump shotgun with a bandolier on the stock completed my arsenal. I pocketed the cash and looked up at Tiny.

"Sorry about this, Tiny, but I'm a little peckish." I had settled down enough to mojo him a little, so I made him knee-walk out into the main aisle. I bit into him just below the left ear and was rewarded with a rush of blood and stimulants rarely felt in my life. Whatever Tiny was on, it was more than just a five-hour energy drink. I felt my muscles sing with blood and stimulants. Between the snack from King before I left the crypt and Tiny's juiced-up blood, I was drinking from the tap a lot more than normal, and I had to admit I liked it. There was just a better flavor to a fresh meal than a pre-packaged one. I drank until I was full, then paused for a second, burped loudly, and took one last sip.

"That's truly disgusting," a voice from behind me said. I whirled around, bringing the shotgun to bear on the intruder.

Greg leaned against the store's front door, a disapproving look on his face. "Did you have to make such a mess of the place, Jimmy?"

"Yes, I did. Tiny here thinks he'll get in less trouble with his boss the more mess I leave behind. Looks like he fought more. How did you get here? And how did you find me?" I wiped my mouth on Tiny's sleeve and walked over to Greg. "Gear up, if you're going with me you're gonna need guns."

"Will do." He started picking pistols out of cases. "And finding you was simple, doofus. I gave you my phone, remember?"

"Yeah, and?" I had no idea what he was babbling about.

"For such a nerd, you are technologically stuck in 1998. I tracked my phone online using King's iPad. Then, I caught the bus over here."

"You can do that? Track a phone, I mean? And how'd you catch a bus? You don't have any cash."

"Any idiot can track a cell phone. And hello, mojo? You really aren't the brains of this operation, are you?"

"Nope," I admitted happily. "I punch things. I think you like to refer to that as the tactical solution. Now we need to get our tactics the hell out of here before the cops show up. So top off the tank on Tiny here; he's on something good."

"You know I don't do drugs. Or humans," Greg said with distaste.

"Drink. I need you at full strength. Or more." He caught the look on my face and drank a little bit from Tiny just to shut me up. A couple of minutes later, Tiny was mojoed into thinking there had been five of us driving motorcycles, and my partner and I were headed for the parking lot.

"What was that guy on? I feel amazing," Greg said.

"I dunno, but I got a feeling we're going to need a lot of amazing before the sun comes up."

Chapter 18

We loaded the backseat of King's pickup with guns, covering them with a layer of fast food wrappers, and rolled north toward where we'd last seen the frat-boy vampires. I had a big pickup truck full of guns and ammo, my best friend riding shotgun, literally, and a belly full of blood. I felt pretty good about my chances for pulling this off and getting Sabrina back in good shape.

It took us the better part of an hour to get across town, wander around campus to find a parking place, make our way back to the construction site where we'd first found Abby, and gear up. Then we crept through the woods as quietly as a pair of clumsy vampires in full combat armament could until the right house came into sight.

"What's the plan?" Greg asked. We stopped just inside the treeline, and the house loomed about fifty yards in front of us. It was just like it had looked on my scouting run, except all the crappy college-kid cars were all gone. When we got closer, I saw the Greek letters over the door proclaiming it as the Beta Beta Beta house, and I chuckled a little.

"What?" Greg whispered.

"The sign," I said. He still looked puzzled, so I took my moment to be the smart one. It didn't happen often, so I tried not to let those opportunities pass me by. "The Greek alphabet doesn't really have a V, so the Beta is as close as it gets for ancient Greek. By calling themselves Beta Beta Beta, they're saying, VVV. Basically they're hanging a sign out saying 'Vampire.' I admire that kind of audacity, even if I plan to gut every one of them."

"You're a weird dude."

"Says the guy with the utility belt."

"Touché. Now, what's the plan?"

I looked over the front of the building and saw no lights on anywhere. "Hard and fast. I go through the front door first and take the upstairs. These old houses usually have a big staircase in the foyer, so I'll head up while you clear the main floor. If you finish the ground floor before I finish the second, you leapfrog me to the third. If everything's clear, we meet in the main foyer to go downstairs together. If everything's not clear, we converge on the trouble and make it dead. Fast. Make sense?"

"Yeah, but why do we wait to go downstairs together?"

"Because that's where I think they'll be if they're home, and there are a bunch of them. We probably can't take them alone, so we should go together. But I don't want to go into the boss fight until we've cleared the rest of the level. Make sense?"

"Yeah, when you make everything sound like *Legend of Zelda*, it makes perfect sense." He chambered a round into his shotgun, I made sure I had a pistol in each hand cocked and locked, and we bolted for the front door. I blew through the door as if it were made of tissue paper and made it up the main staircase in about three long steps. I heard Greg on the first floor, knocking doors off hinges and stomping through rooms. I found myself in a long hallway with doors on both sides, like a scene from a French farce, or a horror movie. There was one door at the end of the hall, and I went for it first, smashing through the old wood like it was nothing.

Oh, come on, you know the drill, it's always the door at the end of the hall. The hero spends all that time checking the rooms on the sides, and there's nothing there. Then he gets to the door at the end of the hall and that's where the bad guy is. Or the girl tied to a chair. Or a bomb. Or, in my case, an empty bathroom. A really disgusting fraternity bathroom at that. By the smell of things in the bathroom, Sabrina had never been there. Neither had bleach. The fixtures were all disgusting, and something in the sink smelled like Ebola, or what one would think Ebola would smell like if one could smell a virus, which I could, and had a morbid curiosity about whether or not they could catch hemorrhagic fevers, which I couldn't.

The other rooms on the second floor were all similarly gross, and all showed the same lack of sexy police detective presence. They were typical dorm rooms, mostly, except with a lot more discarded blood bags than pizza boxes. The bongs and Bob Marley posters were still present in about the same ratio, as well as black-light posters and a ridiculous amount of porn DVDs. Hadn't those guys discovered the internet yet? One whole room was devoted to a small marijuana-growing operation, just a dozen or so four-foot plants, but enough to make me wonder why they'd never been raided by campus police. It also made me wonder if we could get high the normal way. I'd only ever gotten a buzz from booze or stoner's blood, so I had no idea, but was willing to try. I was just going into the last room when I heard Greg's footsteps on the stairs.

"Ground floor's clear," he whispered as he passed my floor. I opened the last door and found a room very different from all the others. It was neatly decorated in modern chrome and black leather, with no pipes, bongs, or rolling papers to be seen. A laptop sat in the center of an IKEA desk, the only personal touch in the room. The screensaver caught my eye as soon as I crossed the threshold. On the screen was a picture of Abby staked to the wall in what used to be our house; three goofy vampires posed in front of her making obscene hand gestures and stupid faces. I sat down in the chair and tapped the touchpad to wake up the computer.

The laptop flickered to life, and a document appeared on the screen. It was a note, addressed to "BusyBody Investigations, Inc." I assumed that was me, so I read it.

"Dear nosy boys, if you're reading this, then you must have gotten our little message at your home last night. She was cute, but a little noisy. Her screams as the silver went into her veins were particularly shrill. If she survived our little barbecue, I do hope you work with her on her wailing. A lower pitch would be much more appealing to the ear. If she didn't, then my condolences. It can be so hard to lose a sibling.

"As for the snack, we thank you. We accept your peace offering of the lovely detective, and will agree to cease all hostilities between our organizations as long as tributes of this quality continue to arrive on a quarterly basis. You can just leave them here in the house for us, and we won't cause you boys any additional harm. There need be no further contact between our organizations as long as you fulfill your duties to us like good vassals. If you refuse, that is, of course, your choice. But please understand that any refusal will be met with my extreme displeasure and may have unfortunate repercussions on certain clerical associates of yours."

It was signed "Sincerely, Professor Wideham." I sat there for a long moment trying to keep my cool, then gave up. I picked up the desk chair and threw it through the wall into the next room. I flipped the bed, tossed a couple of other small pieces of furniture, and ripped the door off the hinges. Greg came running in like a bat out of hell, but paused at the door when he saw I was alone.

"Dude, is there like some invisible monster in there?" he asked from the hall.

"No."

"Then would you like to explain what's going on?"

"No. Read it yourself." I pointed to the computer. He came in, giving me a wide berth as I stood holding the two halves of the door, shoulders heaving with the effort of not going *completely* nuts. He read the letter, chuckled a little, and closed the lid on the laptop.

"What a douche," he said. "Now we're totally going to kill all these assholes, right?"

"Totally."

"Okay, then. Third floor's clear. I got a new laptop out of this

deal, so let's go into the basement and kill a whole lot of bad guys."
He led the way out of the room, then looked back at where I still
stood trying to get my temper under control.

"Hey!" Greg yelled. My head snapped up, and I glared at him.
"Hulk smash down here." He pointed down the stairs, and I followed
him to the basement and my chance to hurt a lot of vampires.

Chapter 19

Except there weren't a lot of vampires in the basement. In fact, there wasn't a lot of anything in the basement, except for the ubiquitous red plastic cups found at every college party in the world. The basement had long since been turned from any lair-type use into a rec room, complete with a pool table, a foosball table, three plasma TVs on the walls, an old Pac-Man game in one corner, and a full bar along one wall. A huge open space, it was littered with couches, chairs, and futons, all covered in magazines and empty blood bags. I did spot a couple of *Rolling Stone* and *High Times* magazines amidst the porn, but those pinnacles of literacy were few. The only concession to lair-dom was a thick metal door with bolts driven through the frame into the concrete foundation of the house. Once that door was locked from the inside, nobody would get in without a wrecking ball.

Greg glanced around the room and immediately started tapping on walls, looking for hollow areas behind them. I tried the more direct approach. I walked over behind the bar and started flipping light switches on the wall. One turned on a blender, resulting in a spray of some truly nasty concoction that for all the world smelled like an O-Negative Margarita. Another, mundanely enough, turned off the lights, causing Greg to trip over an ottoman and swear at me. I enjoyed that so much I did it a couple more times just for fun.

The third switch was the charm. As soon as I flipped it, servos in the door swung it shut and automatically locked the bolts. All the lights in the room went red, making it very difficult for humans to see, but no problem for those of us with undead eyes. The Pac-Man game dropped into the floor on an invisible lift, and a tunnel was revealed behind where it had stood.

"I think we should go that way," I said, leaning carefully on the bar to avoid getting my elbows in the grossness there.

"Showoff," Greg muttered, unclipping a flashlight from his utility belt.

"You're the one with a utility belt, but I'm the showoff?" I followed him into the tunnel.

"If the fangs fit, pal."

"That doesn't even make any sense." I crossed into the tunnel, then froze as the wall slid shut behind me. I looked around for a few seconds, but couldn't find a switch to open the door again.

Greg and I exchanged a look.

I shrugged. "Onward and downward?" My partner, decidedly more grumpy with our escape route cut off, nodded tersely and started down the tunnel.

"Wait!" I hissed.

Greg stopped cold. "What?"

"What if there are booby traps?" I asked, suddenly becoming very interested in the walls and floor of the tunnel.

"What makes you think there are booby traps?"

"These guys are big dorks, right? They've lived up to every stereotype we've been able to think of so far."

"Yeah, so what?"

"Okay, not to put too fine a point on it, but we're big dorks, too," I offered.

"I can see how you might be called that in some circles, but go on."

"Thanks, Captain Spandex. Anyway, if we're big dorks, and they're big dorks, then it makes sense that we share a few common characteristics, right?"

"I still don't include myself in your evaluation, but I'll accept your hypothesis," Greg said patiently.

"The mere fact that you used the word hypothesis proves my hypothesis." He shot me a look, and I went on, "But anyway, that's not the point. Our dorkhood isn't in question here. But think about it, dude. Can you imagine having a secret lair with tunnels underneath it?" The look on his face told me I'd just tapped into the pleasure centers of his brain.

"Ok, now imagine you have a lair with tunnels. Got that image?" From his little smile, his tunnels were full of Playboy Bunnies. "Now, can you imagine any scenario in which you would *not* booby-trap those tunnels?" His smile dropped like Enron stock, and he opened his eyes.

"We gotta be careful, there's no way these tunnels aren't booby-trapped," he said, just as if it had been his idea. He moved forward, slower this time, playing his flashlight along the walls and floor. I just shook my head and followed. I wasn't a huge fan of small spaces, which was why I'd never been much for the coffin stereotype. Give me a California King bed and a vaulted ceiling any day. So skulking along an old tunnel with a ceiling just barely high enough for me to stand upright was nowhere on my list of fun things to do.

The tunnel was dry, at least, and there weren't any apparent spiders. I wasn't afraid of them; I just didn't like them. What did anything need that many legs for, anyway? It was dark, but Greg had

93

a couple of those snap and shake glow sticks in his utility belt, so we each had some light. The floor was packed red clay and looked old, like it had been there a lot longer than the house. I ran my fingers along the rough brickwork and tried to figure out what the place had been before the stoners had made it into their lair.

As if he'd read my mind, Greg whispered, "Underground Railroad." It made perfect sense to me. There were abandoned cellars and passageways all through the South left over from the Civil War, or the War of Northern Aggression, as my redneck Uncle Morris called it. Morris was one of those guys who still used racial epithets in casual conversation and had a confederate flag flying in front of his trailer. He wasn't my favorite uncle by any stretch, but as the saying went, you could pick your nose, but you couldn't pick your family. I was wondering what had ever happened to Uncle Morris when Greg froze in front of me, one hand up, fist closed in a "stop" gesture.

"You realize you were never in the army, right?" I whispered.

"Shut up and be still. There's a trap here."

I looked down and didn't see anything. I was about to say so when I caught a glimpse of it out of the corner of my eye. A thin monofilament line had been stretched across the passageway, going from a hook in one wall to an eyelet mounted opposite. I couldn't see where the line went after it passed through the eyebolt, but I was betting it wasn't attached to anything pleasant.

"You going to disarm that?" I asked.

"This isn't Dungeons & Dragons, dude. Just because I'm wearing black doesn't mean I have the Find & Remove Traps skill."

"Besides, you haven't passed a Dexterity check in this millennium." I chuckled softly when he flipped me off. "What's the plan?"

"I thought we'd try to not break the tripwire. How does that sound?" Greg asked archly.

"Sounds good to me. After you." I gestured grandly down the hall, and he took one exaggerated step over the tripwire. I saw the disturbed soil on the other side of the wire just a hair too late to keep him from stepping on it, then I heard a solid click from the ceiling. I felt a whoosh of air and reached forward to shove Greg to the ground. He sprawled facedown on the dirt, breaking the tripwire with his back foot. Nothing happened there, of course. He'd already triggered the trap when he stepped on the pressure plate on the other side of the dummy tripwire. I spun to the left with blinding speed, but I still wasn't fast enough to save Greg and get out of the way. Being the good friend and hero to the downtrodden, I chose to shove him to the dirt and hope that I survived the booby-trap. When the pole swung out of the ceiling, it caught me square in the gut with a foot-long wooden stake.

Chapter 20

I stood for a long moment staring straight ahead at where my partner lay in the dirt. The stake had passed over his head by a hair and embedded itself about three inches below my solar plexus. I didn't feel anything at first except the impact, but then the pain of the wound started in, and it took all the restraint in the world not to scream bloody murder. A ball of fire exploded in my stomach, and I sagged on the rod that held the stake.

"Greg," I croaked.

"Yeah, what was that all about?" He rolled over angrily, but his eyes went very big when he saw the stake sticking all the way through my skinny frame.

"Would you be a pal and pull this thing out of my stomach?" He nodded and reached up. The stake hung on a rib, and he had to stand up to get enough leverage. Eventually, he put one foot on my chest and pulled, exertion making his face scrunch up and forehead bead with pinkish sweat. With a grinding sound of wood on bone I felt as much as heard, he slowly pulled the stake from my midsection. After what felt like a year, but was probably only a couple of seconds, he got the booby trap out of me, and I collapsed to the tunnel floor.

I lay in the dirt for a few minutes trying to recover as Greg examined the trap. "It's really ingenious, you know," he said, as he swung the pendulum that mere moments before had been embedded in my guts. "The fake trap concealing the real trap. That's some serious Indiana Jones stuff there. And to use a stake on a stick? Genius, I tell you."

I wasn't in a mood to really appreciate the brilliance of the trap that had impaled me, but as I stood, I put a hand on Greg's shoulder, and said, "You're welcome."

"What are you talking about? I saw it coming. I dove out of the way just in time. And besides, the stake got you just under the ribcage; it didn't cause any major damage." When I was finally able to stand up straight, he noticed that the hole in my shirt was level with his heart. Greg sometimes forgot that he was better than half a foot shorter than I was. He looked from my stomach to his chest, gulped deeply, and said, "Thanks," in a very small voice.

We continued down the tunnel, disarming a couple of other traps along the way. They were minor inconveniences, nothing really suited to taking out a vampire—a few poison darts, a couple of spears poking up out of the floor, standard adventure movie gimmicks. After about half an hour of wandering around underground, the tunnel started to widen, and light began to stream in from ahead. The tunnel ended at a high-tech-looking door set into the antique stone walls. A completely anachronistic digital keypad was set into the wall to the right of the door, and what looked like a retinal scanner was right above it.

I tapped for a few minutes, trying out various combinations of UNC-Charlotte important dates on the keypad. Basically, that meant typing every variation of 49 I could come up with, since all I really knew about the college was their prospecting mascot, the 49er. I didn't even know if it had anything to do with gold or with the fact that NC Highway 49 ran right past campus. Given the originality of my home state, I'd put my money on the latter. After watching me for a little while, Greg pulled out his cell phone and a funny cable, pushed me aside, and started his geek-fu on the keypad. He got at least as far as I did but, five minutes later, we were still on the wrong side of the door.

"Scoot back." Greg's frustration made him growl a little. I thought I even saw a hint of fang.

"For what?" I asked, moving back into the tunnel a couple of feet.

"For Plan B." He grabbed the doorframe in both hands and pulled. Greg was really strong, like drop a bus on your head strong, but even so, it was all he could manage to pull that door out of the frame. After healing my stake wound, it was all I could manage to stand upright, so I just stood back and watched as the veins popped out in his neck, and he turned a couple of really odd shades of red, especially given that his blood didn't really move anymore. He got a little movement in the frame, let go, bent his knees to get a lower grip, and wrenched the door out of the wall and over one shoulder. The door turned out to be about eight inches thick and solid metal. It was the wall around it that finally gave way, not the door, and two-hundred-year-old bricks fell in all around us as the tunnel shook from Greg's efforts. He dropped the door off to one side, and I was almost bounced off my feet from the concussion.

"Color me impressed," I said, peering past him into the room beyond the doorway.

"Color me herniated," he gasped, both hands on his knees. "If you see something round on the floor, it's my O-ring. I want that back."

"You're disgusting. Give me your flashlight." The doorway led into a chilly room dimly lit by wall sconces, but the dust from the door's destruction made it hard to see. After a few minutes, I stepped into the room to get a better look. The room was big, with high ceilings. Shelves lined every wall and made aisles all through the room. Every shelf was full of bottles and, when I pulled one from a rack, I realized where we were.

"Greg?" I asked.

"Yeah, what?"

"We're in a wine cellar." Then I took a better look at the bottle in my hand. Instead of a vineyard logo and a year, the label had a name and a photograph of a college-aged girl taped to it. Apparently, I held a bottle of Stephanie, 1963. I took out the cork and sniffed. Sure enough, we were in what had to be Professor Wideham's blood cellar. The blood smelled pretty good, especially for a vintage from the Kennedy era, so I tipped the bottle and took a swig.

It was blood, but it was blood cut with red wine to make it last. Apparently, Wideham had figured out how to mix fermented grape spirits with fresh human spirits to make a pretty tasty treat. It wasn't something I thought would catch on at the local supermarket, but it had a nice bouquet. I drank about half the bottle, then passed it to Greg.

"Top off the tank," I said. He took the bottle and sipped cautiously. "What?" I asked. "I drank it and thought it was fine."

"Yeah," he replied, "but you drink Miller Lite by choice." He finally turned up the bottle and drained it dry, licking his lips afterward.

"Not bad, huh?" I asked.

"Not bad at all. Maybe we'll ask this Professor Wideham, or whatever his name is, how he makes it."

"Before we cut off his head?"

"I think we've got a better shot at an answer if we do it before."

"Good point. So let's find him, get his secret recipe, and cut off his head." I started moving through the stacks of bottled blood wine toward a staircase. Greg followed close behind, and we took the stairs up, pausing at the door atop the staircase.

"What if he's not up there?" Greg whispered.

"Then I eat whoever is up there and make them tell me where to find Wideham."

"Not necessarily in that order," Greg corrected.

"Good point. I get the info, then I eat them. Plan?"

"Plan." With his approval, I turned the knob and stepped out into a very busy restaurant kitchen, surprising two dishwashers and three cooks and making one poor waitress faint dead away.

Greg and I stood stock-still for just a moment, then he pushed past me, holding his wallet in the air and shouting the one word guaranteed to empty most restaurant kitchens. "*Inmigración! Inmigración!*" He walked through the kitchen masquerading as an ICE agent, and the employees scurried like vampires at a tanning bed convention. In about thirteen seconds, we were alone with the unconscious waitress and one very angry head chef.

The chef picked up a big knife and looked like he was about to part Greg's hair with it. I tapped him on the shoulder. He whirled around, looked into my eyes, and froze as I mojoed him into pliability. "Sleep," I said, and he collapsed like a balding sack of potatoes.

"I think we took a wrong turn at Albuquerque, doc," I said in my best Bugs Bunny voice.

"Yeah, me, too. And we need to get out of here before whoever owns this restaurant shows up. Because if they knew about that little wine cellar, they're tied to Wideham. And they might be more than we can handle on our own. This isn't a new setup, and it hasn't happened without some people with some juice knowing about it."

"Yeah, and the last time we tangled with anybody packing that kinda juice, you got thrown off a building." I turned to look for an exit.

"Then it's fortunate for both of you that this restaurant is on the ground floor," the Master of the City said from right behind me.

Chapter 21

"Really?" I said to the air. "This is really happening?"

"What is really happening, Mr. Black?" Tiram asked, obviously not happy to see me in his kitchen. The master vampire was impeccably turned out, again, in a suit that cost more than my car, complete with Italian leather shoes and a pocket square. I didn't even know they still made suits with pocket squares. Of course, he might have had that suit for a generation or two.

"What is happening is that in fifteen years of living here and being what I am, I had no idea you existed. Now I've run into you twice in thirty-six hours, and I'm not happy about it." Greg slunk around behind me, putting as much distance between himself and Tiram as possible. I didn't blame him. It might not have been Tiram who tossed him off a roof, but he certainly had the power to do us serious harm, and I wasn't convinced that Greg had completely healed.

"Somehow, I believe that I may even be less thrilled with our recent level of contact than you are, Mr. Black. Now, why are you here? What were you doing in my wine cellar?" He motioned to the door behind me.

"We were looking for a vampire calling himself Professor Wideham. We followed the tunnels from his lair to your cellar, and came up the stairs hoping to find him here." I figured there was no point in lying about it. It wasn't like we could have come from anywhere else.

"And why are you looking for the professor? I would have thought that the antics of his group would not appeal to you."

"They don't. He and his rejects from *Lost Boys II* torched our home, almost killed one friend of ours, and kidnapped a police officer. We intend to get her back and get a little revenge." I showed a little fang and let my eyes go black around the edges.

Tiram's eyes widened when I mentioned Sabrina's abduction. "That was not authorized, I assure you. Feel free to mete out whatever punishment you feel appropriate under the circumstances." He turned to go into the restaurant. "Now, if you'll excuse me, I have impatient customers that I will now be forced to bespell into thinking they had a delicious meal, and it seems I need to find new kitchen staff as well."

"Hold up there, Spanky." I grabbed his elbow before he got too far away. I heard a sharp intake of breath from Greg, and Tiram turned back to look at me. The little smile that had played across his face since he first caught us in the kitchen was gone, and I felt a little bit of the will of a real Master Vampire hammer at my mind. I pushed past it, throwing him out of my head, and saw his eyes widen.

"Is there something else I can do for you?" he asked after a second.

I let go of his arm. "You said the attack on us wasn't authorized." He nodded. "But something was. What was authorized, and by who?"

"By whom, Mr. Black. Everything that happens in this city is authorized by me, of course. And when Professor Wideham told me you had been spying on him for some days now, I granted him permission to destroy your lair and anyone slow enough to be trapped there. I did not authorize an attempt on the life of a fledgling vampire, nor did I give my blessing to Detective Law's abduction. Now, if you'll excuse me?" He made to turn around again, but I dashed around him, blocking his path.

"How did you know the friend they almost killed was a vampire? And how did you know they took Sabrina?" I got very close to Tiram's face to watch his reaction, but it wasn't at all what I expected. He threw back his head and laughed like I'd told a really funny joke for once.

"Mr. Black, until very recently you have had only three friends in all the world. Mr. Knightwood is here with you. Miss Law is a detective, so it reasons that she was the kidnap victim, and poor Father Maloney is in the hospital. How is the good father, by the way? Please tell him I inquired about his health, won't you? So, given that information, the only person left that you could have possibly stretched to consider a friend is young Miss Lahey, so newly turned by my lovely Krysta. Now that I've proven that I do indeed know more about you than you know about me, or will ever find out about me, may I go on about my business? Or must we have another unpleasant encounter?" He looked up at me without any mojo, without anger, and without the slightest hint of fear. He just stood there, supremely confident that, if there was an "unpleasant encounter," he would come out ahead. I figured he was right, so I got out of his way.

"We're not finished, Tiram," I murmured to his shoulders as he went out into the restaurant.

"Oh, no, Mr. Black. We've only just begun." The swinging door closed behind him.

I turned to Greg and found him leaning heavily on one of the long metal prep tables. He looked paler than normal, and I saw his hands shaking a little as he tried to get himself under control. "You all right, pal? Everything's okay. We didn't have to kill the big bad guy. It's cool." I tried my best to reassure him and, after a long minute or two, he got himself together.

"Yeah, I'm okay. But Jimmy?" He raised his eyes to mine, and I hadn't seen him that scared since we slipped the video camera into the girls' locker room in seventh grade and caught the gym teachers doing the deed in the showers.

"Yeah, bro. What's up?"

"I don't ever want to mess with that guy again. He scares the crap out of me."

"Me, too, Greggy. But I've got a really bad feeling that we're not going to be able to avoid him forever."

"Yeah, I feel it, too. But let's give it a shot, huh?"

"Will do. Now, you got any great ideas about how to find Wideham and his goofballs?"

"Yeah, I've got two. But you're gonna hate both of them." He looked at the floor, and I was pretty sure by his words that I knew what was coming.

"Really?" I asked with a sigh.

"They've got the best sense of what's weird in town, man. Between the four of them, they should have some ideas about where to start looking." Greg still wouldn't look at me, but he had the little smirk bouncing around on his face that I really hated.

"You're probably right." I groaned. "You deal with Her High Priestess-ness, and I'll meet you at the comic shop around eleven. That should give them time to get the civilians safely to bed, right?"

"I doubt it. This is Game Night, so there'll be people there all night. But on the plus side, that means that all three of the guys will be there." He didn't mention that he'd get to try out his new Magic: The Gathering decks, or whatever he played nowadays. I'd always been a nerd, but my partner's geekitude truly knew no boundaries.

"Great. Just what I need after a long week—a dive headfirst into the great unwashed horde of Dorkdom." I turned and headed into the restaurant. I stopped cold at the scene before me. The restaurant was full and gorgeously decorated in a classically elegant style. There were lots of high-backed booths for privacy, marble floors and leather chairs, and not a screaming kid anywhere in sight. The clientele was as high-tone as the decor, Charlotte's version of the glitterati out for a gourmet meal and, by all appearances, everyone was having a grand old time, eating, drinking, laughing, and chatting like all was normal. I even saw a waiter bringing a check to one table, as a man in a tailored dress shirt and tie folded his napkin onto his plate.

His empty plate. His clean, fresh-from-the-kitchen empty plate. What made the scene so bizarre was that there was no food anywhere. The plates were all empty, not a crumb or splash of sauce dirtying up the joint. And all the customers seemed full, or at least seemed to think they were full. I made my way over to where Tiram stood at the host stand near the front door, greeting people and telling them that the restaurant unfortunately was fully committed for the weekend.

"And honestly, we are booked solid for the rest of the month. If you would like to make a reservation for a weekday evening, I believe we have some openings next month. Our weekends are committed until summer, I hate to say." He wore a look that told everyone he didn't really hate to say it at all.

"And how hungry will your clientele be by then?" I mused as I stood next to him.

"If someone hadn't terrorized my entire kitchen staff, tonight's guests would be dining on grand American cuisine rather than simply thinking they were getting their money's worth," he replied, shooting me a dirty look. "Now, please leave my restaurant. You don't meet the dress code."

"Good point. Since I don't meet the dress code, and the amount of human blood in your wine doesn't meet the health code, why don't you loan me an American Express card or two so Greg and I can replenish our wardrobe?" I held out my hand, and the Master of the City gave me a condescending look, then broke into peals of laughter.

"You idiot! You actually pay for things? Just go take whatever you want, then tell the cashier you've paid for it. I haven't dealt with currency in three hundred years. We don't need money, child, we have power. Now, shoo." He waved us out into the night with a peremptory gesture, and we left.

Greg and I stopped out onto the sidewalk. Apparently, we'd covered a couple of miles underground because the restaurant was in an upscale retail development south of the college, complete with high-rise condos, a man-made lake, and a towering Hilton hotel. I looked over at Greg, and said, "Okay, then. Plan stays the same. You go talk with the Wicked Witch of the New South, and I'll meet you at the comic shop in a couple of hours."

"Where are you going?"

"I gotta go see a man about a tumor."

Greg's face fell in spite of my terrible Arnold impersonation, which usually got a chuckle at least. "Give him my best."

"Of course. Now get out of here. I'll see you at the comic shop."

"How am I supposed to get there?" Greg asked.

"Well, you can either eat a cabbie or steal a car. I'm going to go steal a car. Over here." I pointed toward the hotel parking lot. "You steal yours somewhere else."

"When did we become thieves?" Greg asked, a little whiny.

"When the bad guys burned down our house with all the money in it, kidnapped our friend, and blew up our cars." I was getting tired of explaining things as I felt the seconds tick by. Even if Sabrina had made it through the night alive, there was no guarantee that she'd survive another one. We had to find the professor and his students, and soon.

"What do you mean blew up our cars?" Greg was pretty attached to his car, so I'd been holding that tidbit back until he regained a little more of his strength.

"Yeah, when they burned up our place, they torched the garage, too. Your ride is a goner. Sorry." I shrugged.

"Now, I'm pissed. Your car?"

"My car was a piece of crap. Of course, it melted. But I didn't have a decent ride, anyway. I plan to correct that in the immediate future." I started walking off toward the Hilton lot.

"Hey, Jimmy?" Greg called after me.

"What?"

"What are we gonna do about King's truck? He'd be pretty pissed if you left it there." I stopped for a minute, thinking about the grumpy werewolf, and all the guns I'd stolen, and decided just to get a cab back to it.

"I'll take care of it." All visions of swiping a nice Mercedes or Lexus faded from my mind. The night was getting nothing but worse. Not only was I about to go visit one of my best friends in the cancer ward, I had to drive a pickup full of guns to a comic book store. And I still had no idea where Sabrina was being held. But I knew I needed to talk to Mike before I went completely nuts.

Chapter 22

I mojo'd a yuppie into giving me a ride back to campus, and then headed over to the hospital. At least Presbyterian Hospital still had a real person at the parking deck, so I could get out of the lot using my good looks and magical persuasion instead of having to rely on actual cash. The lady at the front desk gestured wildly for a gurney and paged the emergency room as soon as I walked in the door, so I knew I looked my best. I waved my hand in front of her and gave her my best "these are not the droids you're looking for" bit, and she calmed down. I wandered around the hallways for a while looking for the right elevator, then finally made my way up to Mike's room on the fifth floor.

I knocked softly on the door and heard Mike's voice telling me to come in. I stepped into the room to find a nun sitting in the chair next to him, funny headdress and all. She was a healthy woman, as we say in the South, which was to say that she looked like she could throw a cow over one shoulder and cart it off to the butcher's without too much trouble. She had a broad face that managed to look both placid and pinched at the same time. Nuns had always made me uncomfortable, like they might have little microphones hidden inside their headdresses and were receiving orders from the Vatican directly into their ears. Mike gave me a look as if he knew I was about to crack some penguin joke, and put a finger to his lips. I stifled a giggle, mostly because I had been about to crack a penguin joke, and introduced myself as an old friend of Mike's. It was true, too. Mike, Greg, and I grew up together, and had been inseparable as children and all through high school.

We only split up when Mike went away to college, then the seminary, and Greg and I went off to become soulless creatures of the night and undead avengers of the innocent. But Mike looked our age, which was pushing forty, and Greg and I still looked like college kids. That was probably one reason the nun raised an eyebrow when I said we were old friends. The other reason may have had something to do with my deathly pallor, singed jeans, and tattered leather duster. Regardless, she gave me the kind of disapproving look only nuns could truly give, and patted Mike's hand reassuringly before she left.

She paused by the door, looked back at me, and sniffed once before pulling the door closed behind her.

"I don't think Sister Helga likes me," I said, sitting in the room's only chair. I was glad the nun had gone, not just because she freaked me out a little, but because I was tired and didn't want to sit on the end of Mike's bed.

"Maybe she sensed your presence at the top of the food chain, James. Or perhaps she felt that you were an undead abomination. Or maybe you just smell like a barbecue. What in the world happened to you?" Mike struggled to speak, and I handed him a glass of water with a bendy straw. Bendy straws were the only decent thing about hospitals. I'd keep some at home, but they looked silly in beer, didn't work well for blood, and they'd remind me of hospitals.

I gave him the shortened version of my last couple of days, ending with an apology for not being there to check up on him sooner, which he waved off as nonsense. "Given all you've been up to, I'm surprised you remembered me at all, much less thought to have your nice dancer friend look in on me. And let me tell you, he was quite a surprise to Sister Helga," Mike quipped, but his dry chuckle turned into a painful coughing fit, and I helped recline his bed and gave him some more water.

"Jimmy?" He asked when he got his breath back.

"Yeah, pal?"

"What are you doing here?"

"I came to check on you. What else would I be doing?" I protested.

"James, in the past twenty-four hours, you've lost your home, discovered a veritable army of vampires in town that you knew nothing about, watched them almost kill your best friend, and had the woman you love kidnapped. Now don't play games with me, old friend, why are you here?"

"I don't know. I just knew I had to see you." He didn't respond. Mike was good at that, letting the silence build until you broke and had to fill it with something. After a long minute under that gaze, I broke.

"I can't lose her, Mike. I don't know what she is to me, but I can't lose her. It's like, without her, I won't have anything to hold me to what I used to be. Not even you and Greg can do it. I've never felt anything like it, man. When she's around, I'm like a stupid kid again and, when she's gone, it's like…it's like dying all over again. I don't know what I'll be if I can't get her back." I sat there staring at the floor for a minute, waiting for some sage advice I knew wasn't coming.

"You'll be Jimmy Black. A good man with peculiar dietary restrictions. And the heart of a lion."

"But the brain of a scarecrow," I added.

Mike sat up and grabbed my hand, looking me in the eyes and seeing deeper than I usually let anyone see. "Jimmy, we've been friends for a long time, and you know I'm here for you. But this is your battle. Not the battle to save Sabrina, but the one to save yourself if you lose her. You can become a force for great good in the world."

"Or great evil?"

"Yes." He didn't even blink, just held my eyes with his calm gaze. "The boy I grew up with will always be inside you, but the man I know is at a turning point. It's no longer just about what you do, Jimmy. It's as much about how you do it. You have people watching you now, looking to you for guidance."

"Abby," I whispered.

"Yes, Abby. And Greg, too, although he'd never admit it. He follows your lead, and he'll follow you to the gates of Hell itself if you ask. But if you ask, make sure you can come back from those gates. You have to save Sabrina. But you have to save yourself at the same time. You've had a rough couple of days, but you can't let the darkness claim you."

"Yes, Yoda."

"Be serious!" His voice cracked like a whip, and I jerked back. He held my hands fast and kept our eyes locked. "This is real, and the danger is greater than you can imagine. You have a destiny, Jimmy, and it is more than video games, cheap beer, and divorce cases." The crucifix he always wore around his neck became enveloped in a soft white glowing light, and I felt *something* behind his words. Whoever my old friend worked for, he had some serious mystical juice.

"Do you understand?" he asked.

"I think so. Get her back, but do it the right way."

"Exactly. The *how* is as important as the *what*." With that, another coughing fit racked his body, and I helped him lay back down. After a few minutes, his coughing subsided, and he was resting comfortably.

I looked at him lying there looking old and felt for the first time how deep the gulf between my world and the world I in which I had grown up in had become. There I was, immortal, forever young, strong beyond imagining and able to heal from booby traps that should kill anything short of a rhino, and one of my best friends was lying in a bed because his own body had decided to betray him.

"How do you deal with it?" I asked quietly.

For a minute, I thought I'd spoken too softly for human ears, but then Mike answered. "I don't have a choice, Jimmy. Nobody gets out of life alive, not even you."

"I know," I said. "I've been dead for a while."

"That's not what I mean. Whatever happened to you, whatever made you this way, someday it's going to come to an end, too. And then what?"

"What do you mean, then what?"

"What happens to you when you die? Have you given any thought to what you'll say to Saint Peter when you meet him at the gates?"

"I was thinking something along the lines of 'got any beer left?'"

He chuckled again, but his eyes went serious quickly. "That's a good one, Jimmy, but the same question applies to you."

"What question, old man? I got lost thinking about getting drunk with saints."

"How do you deal with it?" Mike asked. "You want to know how I deal with getting old, with the fact that someday I'll die? I deal with it because that's what everybody does. I can look around and find plenty of ways to deal with it, because everyone I see is dealing with it. Except you. How do you deal with that, Jimmy?" His eyes held mine and, for a change, I wasn't the one throwing the mojo around. My old friend had tapped into a higher power of his own, and he was turning some of that insight back on me.

I wasn't really comfortable with it, so I did what I always did– fell back on stupid jokes. "I drink a lot. Porn helps, too. More than you'd think, actually. But mostly I drown my introspection in booze. And with my healing powers, it takes a lot of booze. Now," I said, eager to change the subject. "What did the doctors say? Was the surgery a success?"

"They think they got the entire tumor, yes." There was something in his eyes that belied the good news in his words.

"But?"

"But what?"

"But what's the bad news? What are you trying so hard not to tell me?"

Mike took a deep breath and reached for the water. I gave him another sip, and then put the glass within easy reach. "It's in my lymph nodes. They took one node, but the tests today weren't good. It's spreading, and there's nothing they can do to stop it."

I sat back in my chair and let out a breath I hadn't known I was holding. "How long?"

"Maybe a year, probably less. Maybe eighteen months with a lot of chemo, but without it, probably six to eight months. Sorry, I didn't want to tell you after everything else you've been through."

I was on my feet in a blink, looking for something to hit. "You didn't want to worry me?" I was furious, I was devastated, and I didn't know what I felt. I sat back down, suddenly lacking the energy to stand. "What can I do?"

"Be my friend. Be with me. Don't lose hope, because I won't. And when the time comes, walk away and let me go." There were tears in his eyes, mirroring the ones streaming down my face. I pulled him upright and hugged him to my chest, hard. I cried into his shoulder for longer than anyone should feel comfortable hugging a priest, but finally pulled back to see a big spot of blood on his hospital gown.

"Sorry about that," I said, pointing at the stain. "Don't let vampires cry on your shoulder. It's hell on the wardrobe."

"I'll keep that in mind. But since I only know two crybaby vampires, it shouldn't be much of a problem." I helped him lie back again and covered up the bloodstain until I got out of the room.

"Good point, and we won't talk about all this saltwater on my leather jacket, will we?" I said, wiping off my duster.

"Given the shape that thing's in, it's not like I did any harm."

"Good point. Who else knows?" I asked.

"Just Anna, right now. I haven't informed the parish yet, but they will likely begin training my replacement right away."

"Do you want to tell Greg, or should I?" I couldn't even begin to think about having that conversation, but it was going to have to happen.

"Anna's probably telling him now. She's very sensitive to these kinds of things," Mike said, with a smile.

"Really? You've got something going on with the witch?" Anna was a witchy priestess that had helped us out, with a lot of prodding from Mike, on a couple of cases. I teased him about getting freaky with the Wiccan hottie, but maybe there was more going on than I knew.

"We're very good friends, James. As I'm sure you've heard once or twice, the Church requires her priests to be celibate."

"I've heard a lot of things about Catholic priests, buddy. Some of them even turned out to be true." He laughed again, giving my stupid joke more credit than it deserved. But he was trying to cheer me up, and it was working. We sat in silence for a few minutes, and after a while I noticed that Mike's eyes were closed and his breathing was even again. I sat for a few minutes more, thinking about all the stupid things we had done growing up, and trying not to think about my world without him in it.

After a few minutes, I put my head down and did something I hadn't done since my freshman year of college. I prayed. "God, I don't know if you remember me, or if you can even hear me anymore, given what I am nowadays, but if you're real, and you can hear me, let me just say that this sucks. It's not fair, and it sucks, Okay? I hope you can hear me because I'd really like to give you a piece of my mind right now, but Greg's been telling me for years that I don't have any to spare. But Mike doesn't deserve this, and I don't either, damn it. Why am I going to live forever if you're just going to take the good people away from me? You wanna explain that one, God? You want to tell me why I have to stay stuck in this kid's body forever and watch my friend die?" I lost it there and spent a few more minutes crying before wiping the wasted blood off my cheeks with a paper towel and getting to my feet.

"He hears you," Mike whispered as I turned to go.

I stopped cold. "You weren't supposed to hear all that."

"Kinda hard to sleep with all the blasphemy going on." I heard him chuckle again and smiled a little.

"How do you know?" I asked. "How do you know he hears me?"

"He told me so."

"So he hears me. But does he listen?" I stepped out into the antiseptic hallway and pulled the door closed behind me. My boots squeaked on the polished floors as I made my way to the elevator.

Chapter 23

I pulled into the parking lot beside the comic shop a little after eleven o'clock, and Greg was leaning on the hood of a Porsche convertible. He'd obviously taken the MoC's advice about upgrading his ride to heart, but he didn't seem proud of his wheels. When I got closer, I could tell by the look on his face that Anna had told him about Mike's prognosis, so I did something I never, ever did. I walked up to him, didn't say a word, and gave him a big hug. He and I held each other for a long moment before he pulled away, and we stood there wiping at our eyes.

"If I hear a single gay vampire joke out of you right now, I swear to God, I'll stake you in your sleep," I said, once we had our crap relatively together.

"Deal." Greg's voice was still a little thick with emotion.

I gestured to the back door of the comic shop. "How do you want to do this?"

"Dude, we're not talking about a SWAT entry. We're going into a comic book store on all-night Game Night to talk to some nerds who happen to be friends of mine. I think we can just walk in." Then, he did just that, pulling the door open and walking in to thunderous cries of nerd appreciation. It was kinda like when Norm walked into the bar on *Cheers*, only with no beer and lots of Red Bull. I followed him into the brightly lit back room, where about a dozen folding tables were spread out with all kinds of table, role-playing, and collectible games in progress. There were nerds of all shapes and sizes scattered around the room, from your classic forty-year-old Star Trek geek who lived in his mother's basement to the preteen nerdlets playing Yu-Gi-Oh! or some other unpronounceable card game.

The three guys we needed to talk to were at the head table, moving little lead figurines around in a complicated-looking game. My particular nerd-dom was always focused in a different genre, so I had no idea what they were up to, but Greg fit right in. He was almost a hero to some of the youngest dorklings, having once won the weekly *Magic: The Gathering* tournament for four months straight. His streak probably would never have been broken, but we had a zombie thing come up one night, and he missed that week's game. I wasn't sure he'd forgiven me for that yet.

Nick, the shop owner, sat at the head of the table surrounded by books, dice, and a laminated, colorful dungeon master's screen. His screen looked like it was from the original '70s set and, knowing

Nick, it might have been. Nick was pushing fifty, having started the shop back in the eighties in a desperate attempt to avoid getting a real job. Now, thirty years later, the guy with the ponytail and a t-shirt with D&D dice on the front was a successful businessman, although much of that credit belonged to the clean-cut guy beside him.

Trey was the business guy of the operation, and the one who looked the most out of place in a comic shop. He actually wore shirts with collars most days, but he'd succumbed to the casual-Friday atmosphere and wore a Naval Academy t-shirt.

Dusty was… well, Dusty was an institution more than an employee. He was that skinny guy with the cactus-looking chin beard and an encyclopedic knowledge of comics that was a little creepy in the depth and breadth of it. He knew as much about R. Crumb and *Maus* as he did about *Captain America* and *Green Lantern*, and would happily go for hours on the difference in artistic styles between John Byrne and Neal Adams. Dusty was always working on a project of his own, talking about leaving the store to make his own art, but still showing up for work every day.

These were the guys we on whom we had pinned our hopes of finding Sabrina. I felt the ball of dread in my stomach growing with every step closer to their gaming table, and it didn't shrink at all when Nick looked up over his DM screen and shouted, "Greg! Come for my rematch? We're in the middle of an adventure right now, but go ahead and warm up on the vermin, and I'll get to you in a couple hours!" I was pretty sure he included me in the "vermin" remark, but he'd waved his arm over to where a bunch of kids were playing cards.

"Nick, I need your help," Greg said quietly, and the buzz of conversation halted immediately. Every head in the place turned to Greg and Nick, as the two superstars of their little universe got ready for a team-up. It was like a real-life crossover issue for Charlotte's nerd set.

Nick leaned back in his chair, affecting a Godfather posture, and said "What can I do for you, Greg? Whatever it is, I'm sure we can come to some sort of an… arrangement." He smiled a slow smile, and I remembered Greg mentioning that Nick had been after a few of his more prized comics for the last few years.

"We don't have time for this," I muttered to Greg, keeping my voice out of the range of human hearing. Out of the corner of my eye, I did notice one teenager prick up his ears at the threat in my tone. I looked at him, and he ducked his head and started throwing decks of cards into a backpack. *Wonder what he is?* I thought, and filed his face away for future reference.

"Be cool. If it looks like he's going to be a real ass about helping us, you can eat him. But let me try to talk first," Greg whispered back.

"Fine, but talk fast. We're running out of moonlight, and I'd kinda like to check on Abby before we go chasing our next lead."

"What, you don't trust King?" Greg looked a little alarmed.

"Dude, I don't trust anybody. But I'm more worried about *her* killing *him,* than vice versa. All I need on my hands is a vampire werewolf. And no, that would not be cool," I added when I saw the gleam in his eyes.

"So what do you need, Gregory? I'm in the middle of a new *Rogue Mage* campaign here." Nick always used full names when he was being a jerk. I never got it.

"Is there somewhere we can speak privately?" I asked. Nick turned on me what he obviously thought of as his best demeaning stare, the kind of look that made preteen boys quail with fear when questioning the valuation of a comic. It didn't have a lot of effect on me. Face certain death enough times, especially if you really did end up dead, and the normal mortal intimidation techniques just didn't work like they used to.

"Anything you have to say to me, you may say in front of my minions and my legions of adoring admirers." Nick made what I was sure looked like a grand gesture in the movie in his mind, but in real life looked like he swung a scrawny arm around his head in a spastic flurry of motion.

"We'd really rather do this in private," I insisted.

"Greg, tell your rude friend that I'm not leaving my game." Nick folded his arms in front of his equally skinny chest.

"Okay, pal. Your disaster." I moved to the front of the room where everyone could see me clearly. "Hey, everybody!" I clapped my hands. Every head in the place spun around, and all eyes were on me. Uber-geeks weren't that accustomed to being addressed, so when given the opportunity for some attention, they got a little deer-in-the-headlights look about them.

When I had everyone's attention, I said, "You will sleep for the next thirty minutes. You will not notice the loss of time. When you wake up, you will swear off chocolate and drink lots of water for the next six months. Soda will taste like cardboard, and you will have no appetite for sweets or fried food. Except for you three." I waved my arm at Dusty, Trey, and Nick. "You three are off the hook. Now sleep."

Every head except for the Three Stooges dropped to the gaming tables with a sound like an unripe watermelon dropped from a bridge onto a passing truck. I actually knew exactly what that sounded like from a past experience. Nick and his cohorts were still awake and aware, and a little freaked out.

"What was that, some kind of mass hypnosis?" Trey asked.

"Yeah, something like that," I said.

"What was the bit about chocolate and fried food?" Dusty asked.

"I figured if I had the chance to help these poor schmucks get a date for once in their lives, may as well take it," I replied. "Now, guys, we need your help. I don't know exactly what Greg has told you about us, and I don't care. For tonight, we're in a hurry, and we need your help." They looked back at me blankly, giving me their best ignorant stares, so I knew Greg had spilled the beans.

"Go ahead, fellas, he knows the deal," Greg said, and the nerd brigade sprang into confused action. Nick ran into the store and came back with a backpack and a huge flashlight. Trey whipped out a laptop and fired up a browser window, while Dusty just sat there looking a little confused.

"I'm ready, team!" Nick announced, brandishing his flashlight like a lightsaber.

"I think right now we need a little more of Trey's kind of help and a little less charging blindly into the fight," Greg said gently. Nick looked crestfallen and put his flashlight through his belt.

I patted him on a shoulder and moved around behind Trey. "Don't sweat it. That's my first instinct, too. Unfortunately, that's kinda what got us into this mess."

"What am I looking for?" Trey asked, fingers twitching over the keys.

"We're looking for a vampire who calls himself Professor Wideham and his gang of bloodsuckers over by the college. We went to their main lair tonight, but it was abandoned. So we need to figure out this guy's identity and where he might be hiding out," Greg said, leaning over Trey's shoulder.

"Oh, is that all?" Dusty said, coming out of his semi-trance and looking around.

"What do you mean, is that all?" I asked him. Talking to Dusty was always a little like talking to Rain Man. I never knew whether what came out was going to be pure gold or pure crap, and it usually took a long time to figure out which.

"I know Dr. Wideham. That guy's got one of the best Gold and Silver Age collections in the state! He used to come in here all the time on Game Night, but he never played anything, just looked through the back issues for hours. Said it was the only time he could make it into the store. He knows everything there is to know about Silver Age Justice League, and Flash in particular." Dusty looked pleased with himself, kind of like the look a cat would have when he dropped a dead mouse at his owner's feet.

"That's great, D. But do you know where to find him? Like we said, the frat house was empty." Greg spoke softly, so as not to spook the savant.

"Yeah, man. He hasn't lived there in years, since one of the guys messed up his Justice League Number 77. Took him like three years to replace that book, so he took all his stuff and moved into a place of his own." Dusty's gaze fogged with recollections of Silver Age Justice League issues, and Greg had to snap his fingers to bring him back.

"Sorry, man," Dusty apologized.

"It's okay, D. Where does he live now?" I asked.

"Who?" Dusty looked confused again, and I was afraid I was going to eat him if we didn't get to the point sometime soon.

"Dr. Wideham. Where does the Professor live, Dusty?" I spoke slowly, using small words.

"Oh, I don't know off the top of my head, man. Somewhere up near the university, but not with the other guys anymore. Not since they—"

I cut him off. "Ruined his Justice League Number 77, we know. But how would you get in touch with him if you found a rare comic that you thought he'd want to see or maybe buy?" I thought if I used his terms, maybe that would get Dusty down out of the clouds for a couple of precious seconds.

"Oh. I've got his address in the computer, man. Why didn't you ask?" He wandered off toward the computer at the front of the store, shaking his head.

"Go with him. Make sure he doesn't get lost," I told Greg with my face in my palm. He came back a few minutes later with a slip of paper.

"Got it. Two known addresses for Dr. Wideham, who sometimes uses the name John Jones for anonymous auction-type stuff." He grinned when he said the name, like I should recognize it.

"I give up. Who is John Jones?"

"The secret identity of The Martian Manhunter, J'onn J'onnz, dude! This guy is a *total* Justice League nerd." Greg used a tone that said I needed to turn in my nerd card for not knowing that one. I still didn't get it, but I nodded enough to get him to leave.

We were almost to the back door of the shop when I heard

Dusty's voice coming from the cash register. "Hey, man, if you like, exterminate him, can I have his comics?"

Chapter 24

I grabbed the scrap of paper with Wideham's addresses on it from Greg as we walked to the car. I stopped cold.

He kept going for a couple of seconds before he noticed I wasn't with him anymore. "What's up?" he asked, jogging back to where I stood.

"Well, we don't have to worry about which address he'll be at." I pointed to the paper.

"Why's that?" Greg asked.

"Nothing about these addresses looks familiar to you?" I asked, waving the paper in front of his face.

"Not at that speed, no." He grabbed it from me and looked closely at the numbers Dusty had scrawled. After a couple of seconds, it hit him. "Oh, crap."

"Yeah. Oh, crap is right. Think it's a coincidence that this Professor character has an apartment in the same building the Master of the City has a fancy restaurant?" I took the paper from him and threw it over my shoulder.

"Not so much. So, what do we do?" Greg didn't look too keen on any more run-ins with the Master, and truth be told, I wasn't thrilled with the idea either. But Sabrina needed my help, so I swallowed hard, got in the truck, and cranked the engine.

"We don't do anything tonight. We've only got a couple hours left until dawn, and I'd bet anything that Tiram has told Professor Wideham all about our little visit by now. We need to hole up someplace and make a plan. And I know just the place." I pulled the truck into traffic and started heading back toward the campus. Greg looked at me quizzically, but I just smiled and dug out the phone I'd swiped from Tiny back at the pawn shop.

King answered after a couple of rings. "I almost didn't answer, but I figured not knowing the number doesn't mean much around here."

"Yeah, sorry about that. I'm tough on cell phones. This one's a loaner."

"Does the owner have any use for a cell phone anymore?" the werewolf asked.

I stared at the phone for a minute in confusion, then the meaning of his words sunk in. "Dude! I did not eat the last guy that had this number. Seriously! Now meet us at the back entrance to the church in ten minutes. I found a place for us to crash. We'll hole up there for the day and go get this Professor chump as soon as the sun goes down." I hung up and looked over at Greg. He was looking at me like I was insane, which wasn't completely out of the question.

"What?" I asked innocently.

"Really? You have to ask?"

"It'll be fine. It's empty, has a huge basement, and wi-fi. What more can you ask for?" I tried to keep my eyes on the road, but it was tough holding back my laughter.

"If I can't find a place that hasn't been the lair of evil vampires, I think I'd settle for someplace that didn't reek of stale beer and date-rape drugs," Greg grumbled, as we pulled the truck into the church and loaded up the others. Abby and I took the back seat, and we headed for the frat house that had, until recently, been the lair for Wideham and his gang of stoner vampires. One good thing about taking over an evil vampire's property—there was bound to be blood in the crisper. And if it was a vamp lair that doubled as a frat house, then there was going to be blood and beer. And that was what made unlife worth unliving.

Greg, Abby, and I settled in to while away the day, and King went out to try and dig up some more leads on Krysta. I'd forgotten about her in my worry over Sabrina, but he hadn't. The look in his eyes when he said where he was going told me he wouldn't be forgetting Krysta any time soon. I resolved again not to ask what she'd done to get under his fur like that. Because no matter how curious I was, I didn't need any other drama rolling around in my head.

By midmorning, Greg and Abby were fast asleep, and I was safely brooding in the basement. I tried to sleep, but images of Sabrina kept flashing on the inside of my eyelids. Sabrina throwing me over her shoulder as we sparred. Sabrina kicking me in the face in a practice bout. Sabrina waking me up with a stake to my heart. It was funny the things that warmed my heart about her.

A few minutes after sundown, I heard King's truck pull up. I got up and checked my weapons for the twenty-fifth time. Greg and Abby came out armed to the teeth, and we loaded into the pickup to head over for a little conversation with Professor Wideham—the kind of conversation that usually ended up with one party bleeding a lot. I had King make a quick stop before we headed over to the fight, just to see if there was anything salvageable at our old apartment. We drove right through the yellow police tape, and Greg hopped out, running straight to the burned-out shell of the garage. His beloved 1967 GTO was nothing but a frame on melted tires, barely enough left to recognize it for the badass muscle car it had once been.

I left him to his grief and jumped down into the remnants of the apartment to poke around. Not much was left standing, just the major support beams and a couple of walls. The cheapo desk Greg's computer had lived on had made it out almost unscathed, confirming my belief that particle board was made of magical components to reduce cost and increase weight. I wandered dumbly through the den and kitchen that had been my home for more than a dozen years, thinking about the good times we'd had there. I made my way into what used to be my bedroom, kicking debris out of the way, until I saw a glint of metal. I reached down and picked up the sword that had come back from FairyLand with me, still in its leather scabbard. The scabbard and sword belt seemed none the worse for wear and, when I drew the sword, the blade gleamed just as brightly as when I had used it to fight trolls in the castle of the Fairy Queen. Yeah, really. That happened, too. I belted it on, thinking there was always room for one more bladed implement, and started to climb out of the hole.

I paused by what used to be our kitchen and kicked over the refrigerator. The door fell open, spilling exploded beer bottles and bags of boiled blood onto the ground. Our safe was intact, so I yelled up to Greg for the combination. I didn't understand why he picked 11-10-60, and didn't care, because when I pulled the door open, there were stacks of cash and a bag full of fake IDs and credit cards for both of us. I stuffed whatever would fit into my pockets and carried the rest up to the truck.

"Nice haul," King said.

"Well, you always forget something when you go on a trip, right?"

"Yeah, but it's not always a hundred grand and half a dozen passports."

"Be prepared."

"You were no Boy Scout," Abby said from the back seat.

"Yeah, but since the fratboys that staked you to our wall also took your Victoria's Secret money, I think you're glad I've drunk a couple of Eagle Scouts in my day." I gave Greg another moment or two to mourn his car, then waved him back into the truck.

"What's the plan?" Greg asked, as he slid into the backseat of the pickup.

I looked back at him. "We go get our friend back. And kill anything that tries to get in our way. Agreed?"

"Agreed. And maybe get a little revenge for what they did to Maybellene."

"You called your car Maybellene? Like the makeup?" Abby asked.

"No, like the old song, you know?"

"No. I don't. And why do guys have this obsession with naming things, anyway?"

"We are so not having this conversation." Greg turned to look out the window, and we rode the rest of the way in silence. That worked for me because I needed more time to think about what they might be doing to Sabrina. Sure, I did. I wasn't crazy about bringing Abby in if we were going to fight a bunch of vamps, but we'd seen how well leaving her behind had worked. We parked at the far end of the front parking lot, and I gathered everybody in to explain what little plan I'd devised.

"Here's the deal. We're going in blind, with no idea what's in there waiting for us. Judging from the traps laid out around the frat house, it seems like our friend is a wee bit security-conscious, as well he should be. So we don't know if Sabrina's in there, or where she's being held, and how many bad guys we might have to face to get to her."

"So, it's hopeless?" Abby asked.

"Well, if we weren't already dead, I wouldn't have a lot of confidence in our coming out of this alive. But since that matters less to us than to a lot of people, I think we'll be okay." I didn't think anything of the sort, and I could tell from the nod King gave me that he knew it. But Abby was scared enough, so there was no point in giving her anything else to worry about. "Now, we have enough firepower here to seriously ruin a vampire's day, but you have to know what you're doing."

"I've never even held a gun before," Abby said, starting to shake again.

"That's why you're on the shotgun. Point, pull the trigger, and rack the slide. Lather, rinse, repeat. Anything in front of you will have a tough time getting through all the lead you'll be slinging." I handed her a 12-gauge and a couple of boxes of ammo. "When you're out, put shells in here. If you run out of time, use it like a baseball bat."

King was already neck-deep in the stack of guns I'd swiped from the pawnshop. He grabbed an AR-15 and a pair of 9mm handguns.

"I don't know if I have ammo for that rifle, King," I protested.

"I do." He reached into a toolbox bolted to the bed of the truck and pulled out a box of rifle shells.

"But you don't carry a gun?" Abby asked.

"Ammo isn't illegal anywhere, darlin.' Guns are a different

story. It's not usually a big deal to pick one up wherever I am, but it's not something I want to have in the truck if I get pulled over by a nervous state trooper." He took a few magazines, then put one in the gun and the others in his back pockets.

Greg got out of the truck and helped himself to a couple of pistols and a shotgun. I took another AR-15 and started loading my own clips. After a few minutes, we were as ready as we were going to get.

I looked at my motley crew. "I don't know if we'll find anything. Might be all that happens is we scare the crap out of a few bankers and move on to the next house on our list. Or we might find a nest of vamps ready to kill us all. But..." I ran out of words trying to let them know how important it was to go in and get Sabrina to safety.

Greg stepped up and put a hand on my shoulder. "Let's go get her back." We all nodded and headed toward the front door, bristling with fangs, firearms, and bad attitude.

The entrance to the restaurant was separate from the apartment lobby, so we had at least a passing chance of getting upstairs without the Master knowing about it. I walked in the front door and strode to the security desk as if I owned the place.

"Can I help you, sir?" This came from a polite blond kid with a crew cut and some fierce acne.

I leaned my elbows on the counter and locked eyes with him. "Everything is normal. Nothing out of the ordinary has happened tonight. You lost your security badge somewhere." I reached out and snatched the magnetic ID card from around his neck. "You never saw anyone except residents and guests." The mesmerized guard nodded slowly, and King took a second to strip down to his undies before shifting into his tall, dark, and furry form. I thought I saw Abby lick her lips at the werewolf's trim form, but pushed any comment aside for later as we got in the elevator.

"We know his apartment number, so that's the easy part. King and I will go in first. Greg, you follow five seconds later with Abby." They all nodded, and I took a deep, and completely unnecessary, breath as the elevator dinged at the penthouse level. We crossed the foyer to Wideham's door, King on my heels and the others about twenty feet behind.

"What's the plan?" he whispered.

"I'm making it up as I go along. Can you hear anything?"

"No, but gimme a second." He put his nose to the hinge side of the door and sniffed deeply. He bent over and repeated the process at the bottom of the door, then stood back up. "There are at least two vampires on the other side of the door, both packing."

"How?" I started to ask, but he waved me off.

"Stale blood and gunpowder. How do we go?"

"Fast. I've got the left."

King reared back with one huge foot and kicked the door off its hinges. He and I were the first ones through, and what we saw in there made us both stop cold. There were about a dozen vampires in various states of undress, sleepwear, and drug-induced stupor. But my eyes locked on Sabrina. She was tied to a straight-backed kitchen chair with a skinny vampire standing over her. He didn't look like any professor I'd ever seen, and he didn't exude that sense of power over the other vampires that would make me think he was their creator, so I pegged him for just another punk bloodsucker in a Widespread Panic t-shirt.

"Make another move, and I'll drain her before you can blink," the vamp said. "She's pretty empty already, what with my boys here snacking on her for the past couple of days. It shouldn't take more than another nibble or two, and she'll never need sunscreen again. So put down your weapons, and let's pretend to be civilized."

I kneeled and laid my rifle on the carpet. As he smirked at me, I reached behind my back, grabbed the .357 revolver I had tucked into my belt, and shot him once in each eye.

Chapter 25

The vampires reacted to stress a lot like humans, especially the ones that hadn't been dead for very long. It wasn't surprising, since we started off as human, and no one gave us a vampire behavior manual when we were turned. So it wasn't unexpected when about a third of the vamps took off at a dead run once the shooting started, because that was what about a third of humans would do. Another third sat there like morons and screamed, which made them particularly easy to dispatch, but the final third presented a little more trouble.

I shot the three screamers in their foreheads. The large-caliber bullets wouldn't kill them since they weren't silver, but they weren't going to be any threat for the rest of the night. I tossed the pistol aside and bent down to pick up my rifle again. Before I could raise it, I heard the roar of a shotgun and felt the breeze as pellets flew over my back. I dropped flat onto my stomach and rolled over to see Abby standing over me, barrel smoking. Her eyes were huge, and I followed her gaze to where a vampire lay in two pieces on the tattered rug. A 12-gauge at eight feet made a big mess, and Abby had gotten the guy full in the gut.

"I think that counts as decapitation," I said from the floor, and reached a hand up to Abby. She helped me stand, and we looked around the room. Of the four vampires who had attacked when I shot the first guy, all but one was down. Greg had emptied a 9mm magazine in one guy's face, King had ripped one vampire's throat out with his bare hands, and a third poor bastard was standing there looking at us with a kitchen cleaver in his hand.

I took one step toward him, raised my AR-15, and said, "You should run now." He apparently thought that was good advice because he dropped the cleaver and ran straight through the living room window. His legs never stopped moving, and I wondered idly if he'd learn how to fly before he hit the ground. I looked out at where he lay crumpled on the hood of a burgundy Jetta. *Nope. Guess not.*

Greg was already at Sabrina's side, kneeling by her legs and untying her. I made my way across the room and froze as her head snapped up. She focused on me for the first time since we'd gotten there. Her eyes were wild, unfocused, and she let out a shrill scream when she saw my fangs. She tried to pull away, but was still tied to the chair with one leg, so all she managed was to topple over with her hands still bound behind her.

I caught her before she hit the floor, cradling her head and whispering nonsense sounds, trying to comfort her as Greg got her other leg free. As soon as she had the use of her hands, she started to pummel me, trying to get away. I held her tightly to my chest, letting her beat on me until her arms got tired. Gradually, the shrieks turned to sobs, and the pounding on my chest became slower until she draped both arms around my neck and buried her face into my shoulder, sobbing and panting out sounds more than actual words. I sat down on the floor with a thump and just held her as her hot tears soaked my shirt. If the comforting thing kept up, I was going to have to start wearing rubber t-shirts. I sat there for several minutes, not moving, just holding her, and letting her babble at me.

After a couple of minutes, her breathing slowed, and she managed to pull away and look around. She scooted back a little when she caught sight of King, who was still seven feet of hair and bloody claws. But she was a woman who'd battled trolls in a cage fight; she wasn't going to be frightened of a little wolfman for long.

She looked around the room at the dead and writhing vampires, and then looked back at me.

"You made a mess of this place. The cops will probably be here soon." She wiped her eyes, obviously trying to regain her composure.

"I doubt that sincerely, Ms. Law. As a matter of fact, they will not be responding to any calls in this part of town for the next several hours." Sabrina let out a shrill whimper and backed away from the voice as I leapt to my feet.

A tall, well-dressed vampire stood in the remains of the doorway. He exuded class and breeding, things I'd read about in books but never really seen much of. His long brown hair was pulled back into a neat ponytail, and he picked his way through the debris as he came toward me, careful not to soil the cuffs of his suit pants. I hated him on sight.

"Professor Wideham, I presume?" I stepped forward, cutting off his view of Sabrina, and held out my hand.

He shook my hand and nodded. "Precisely." I decided if he called me "my dear Watson" I'd just rip his head off and skip the banter. "To what do I owe the unique pleasure of your company this evening?"

"We're just here to retrieve our friend. Oh, and to cut off your head and crap down your neck. That's all," Greg said from beside me. He was pretty fast for a fat dude.

"I don't think that will be necessary, Mr. Knightwood. After all, we have such mutual affection for one of my students. Come in, my dear. Say hello to your big brother." He waved an arm and a pretty young girl, about the right age for a college senior, came into the room. I heard a sharp intake of breath from beside me and knew that not everybody in the room would be walking out under their own power. The girl had dark hair, a slightly round face, and blue eyes. It didn't take a genius to see the family resemblance. After all, she looked exactly like Greg. If he had been a chick. And not fat. And alive.

Emily had been six when we were turned. She was the cutest little kid, and Greg had doted on her. Letting her believe he was dead had been the hardest thing he'd had to do since being turned, and now there she stood. She stopped beside the elder vamp, her eyes glazed.

"Let her go. She's got nothing to do with this." Greg's voice was low and dangerous and, when I looked over at him, I saw something in his eyes I'd never seen before. My best friend was ready to kill somebody, and in the most painful way imaginable.

"Oh, but she has everything to do with this, Mr. Knightwood. After all, she's missed you terribly. She talks about her dearly departed brother in all of our advising sessions. She's really very bright, you know. It would be such a waste if anything were to happen to her." He put a hand on her shoulder, but all I saw was how close it was to her neck. There was no way any of us could get to her before the monster snapped it like a twig.

A heavy silence fell over the room. I almost heard us all thinking, trying to come up with a plan that didn't end with Emily dead, or worse. After an eternity or two, I said "What do you want?"

"Well, I seem to be in need of a new door, for starters," Wideham said calmly.

"And we're short a place to live. I think we're probably even on that count, Teach." I sat down on the remains of the sofa and put my feet up on the coffee table. It seemed like he was more into talking than fighting at that moment, and anything I could do to back Greg down a hair was probably a good move on my part.

"Yes, well, that was unfortunate. But you did initiate the hostilities." He flipped an armchair upright and sat in it. Emily knelt at his side like an obedient pet. I caught Greg's eye and gave him what I hoped he took for a *chill out, I have an idea* look. But for all I knew, it just looked like I had to sneeze. Either way, he backed up a step, and so did King.

"What are you talking about? We didn't even know you existed until I caught your scent where Krysta killed Abby." I leaned forward, really confused. Oddly enough, that was a little comforting. When you spent as much time confused as I did, it became kind of your status quo. Without a clue what was going on, I felt a lot more normal.

"You mean, where Krysta left young Abigail as an offering to me. A gracious gift in exchange for passage through my territory."

Suddenly, it made a lot more sense.

"I get it now. Krysta hunted on your turf, so she had to make it right. And the way to do that was to give you Abby." I leaned back again, waving at Abby to be quiet. Her twenty-something college student idealist feminist sensibilities had been offended, so I looked up at her. "It's got nothing to do with you being a girl, sweetheart. It's more about the fact that you were a meal. Krysta turned you, and the Prof here was supposed to find you and make you part of his little posse here."

"Exactly, Mr. Black. Perhaps you aren't as much an idiot as you appear," Wideham said, smiling as he played with Emily's hair.

"I'm not enough of an idiot to keep putting my hands on Greg's sister with both of us in the room, that's for sure." His hand froze, and his eyes flicked over to Greg. Greg hadn't moved, but that was all the distraction I needed.

I kicked the coffee table up into the air, and yelled, "Grab her!" to King. The big werewolf was almost vamp-fast, and had been waiting for my signal. He snatched Emily up and bolted for the door. A young vampire came in from the hallway to intercept him and found himself suddenly decapitated by one sweep of King's massive claws. The last thing he saw was his body falling as his head bounced off the doorjamb. King got Emily out of the room and didn't stop moving as Greg, Abby, and I encircled the older vamp.

"Very well played, children. But now it's time for the grownups to be in charge again. So *sleep.*" I felt the mojo in his words roll over me, and I watched Sabrina sag bonelessly to the floor. Abby fought it, but she was no match for the older vampire's mind. The couple of Wideham's minions that had managed to regain their feet went out as well, and Greg and I were left alone with the master vampire.

Chapter 26

"Should we do this the easy way," I asked Greg, "or the hard way?"

"I vote the hard way," my partner said, as he cracked his knuckles. I drew the fairy sword and passed it over to him. He had a lot more *Lord of the Rings* fetish than I did. I just wanted to punch the bad guy's heart out through his spine, but I figured Greg wanted to do things with a little more flair.

"Boys, do you really think you can match my power, my intellect, my experience?" Wideham was trying to maneuver us so we had our backs to the shattered window, but I didn't budge. Greg didn't either, and that was a lot of bulk to move.

"Nope," I said. "But I think we've got you crushed on witty banter and dashing good looks." I launched myself at the vampire, but he dodged easily. Of course, when he did, he dodged right into Greg's meaty fist. I heard a sound like a lot of bubble wrap popping all at once. "And the good-looks gulf just gets wider. I'm pretty sure that's the sound of a crushed nose."

The Professor let out a snarl and dove for me, almost taking flight in his rage. I easily sidestepped, then caught one arm as he went past. It wasn't exactly Judo, more the product of watching a lot of Saturday afternoon Bruce Lee movies, but it was enough to toss him into a wall. More drywall dust filled the room, and Wideham pulled himself out of the architecture. He turned to us, holding up both hands in a placating gesture.

"Now, boys, why can't we be friends? You can join my fraternity, live in our house with us. I hear you need a place to live. We could hunt together, pick up college girls together. Dine together." I heard the creak of the ruined floor and dropped straight down, just barely avoiding the machete swinging at my throat from behind. Greg wasn't as quick, but he didn't have to be. The difference in our heights once again proved his salvation, as the blade whistled right over his head and buried itself into a wall.

I stood up and found myself face to face with maybe the single largest vampire I had ever seen. Six-foot-ten, if he was an inch, the bearded blonde behemoth looked every bit of a *Thor* stunt double, only with fangs and uber-white skin. He looked down at me, something that almost never happened to me, and grinned. That was twice in one week I'd been the short guy in a fight, and I didn't like it one bit. I smiled a sickly smile, and mumbled, "Nice giant, don't eat the skinny one."

Thor punched me in the gut, and I folded like an origami swan. I wasn't gasping for air, exactly, more lying on the ground flopping around like a fish, a fish in a lot of pain. I looked up to see Thor smiling down at me like the world's stupidest statue, then I rolled to one side to avoid what must have been a size thirty-eight shoe crashing towards my head. The whole room shook as Thor stomped partway through the ceiling of the floor below us.

I came to my feet with a pistol in each hand and a lopsided grin on my face. "Now, Thor, nobody has to die tonight," I said, going for the reasonable approach.

Thor just looked at me and laughed as he pulled a shotgun out of the back of his pants. Seriously, the dude had a sawed-off shotgun in the waistband of his pants as if it were a .38. He pointed it at my face, and said, "Wrong, dork. You have to die tonight." He flashed me a vicious grin and pulled the trigger.

The shotgun boomed loud in the small apartment, and buckshot blew out even more glass, but I was long out of the way before Thor pulled the trigger. I was fast—crazy fast. I tapped the behemoth on the shoulder and, when he turned around, there was a 9mm pistol pressed against each cheekbone.

"Now put the gun down, and jump out the window, or I'm repainting this place in Giant Brain Gray." Thor did as I asked, and I heard a sickening crash from below as he landed on a vehicle and blew every piece of glass out of the frames.

I turned to where Wideham stood in the middle of the room. He hadn't budged through our whole encounter with his bruiser, just stood there watching. Greg had a gun in his non-sword hand, but something told me he wasn't going to have any more luck shooting the Professor than Thor had shooting me.

"Well played, gentlemen, well played," Wideham said, stepping forward with a smile. Greg pulled back the hammer on his pistol, but then the older vampire's hand blurred and the gun simply wasn't there anymore. I heard another small crash outside, and then heard the gun go off down in the parking lot.

"I thought I was fast," I murmured, looking at the master vamp with new respect.

"You are, for one so young. But I have been haunting institutions of higher learning since I entered Cambridge with little Francis Bacon. I have, as you say, learned a thing or two along the way. And one of those things is the art of the retreat." With that, he bolted for the open door, only to find Greg standing there. I never even saw my partner move, he was just *there*. Wideham looked at Greg's stony face, then at the golden sword, and stepped backward into the room. He turned to make a dash for the open window, but I blocked his escape.

"I don't want to fight you boys; someone might get hurt." The master vampire held up his hands placatingly as his eyes scanned the room for another way out. Greg tested the edge of Milandra's sword on his thumb, licking the thin line of blood that appeared. I never understood how that sword stayed so sharp. I only ever used it in sparring, but it never got dull. That might be a very good thing before the night was over.

"I think you're right, Professor. Somebody's going to get hurt." Greg's eyes were flat, a slight tremor in his hands the only hint at the rage he fought to hold back.

The old vampire looked over at me, pleading. "Mr. Black, please restrain your friend. There is no need for further violence, is there? I can leave town, never return. Find a new place to hunt, a new university in which to lecture. I give you my word I shall never return to Charlotte."

"You're right," Greg said, "You won't." And in a blinding lunge, he thrust the sword through Wideham's heart. The sword wasn't wood or silver, but it seemed to have the desired effect anyway. The blade slid out the back of the elder vampire's chest, and then the whole thing started to glow with a bright purple light. The Professor's body glowed in turn, and the same purple light came flooding out of his eyes, ears, nose, and mouth. In a matter of seconds, his entire body was consumed with blinding lavender light and then, quicker than a blink, the light was gone. And so was Dr. Wideham. There was a small pile of clothing covered in purple dust on the floor where he had stood, and the sword in Greg's hand was just an ordinary, but very sharp, and apparently ridiculously magical, blade again.

I reached out very carefully, took the sword from him and slid it back into the sheath on my hip. He looked at the pile of dust on the floor, raised a foot, and kicked it all over the rug. "Nobody messes with my baby sister." Then he turned and walked slowly toward the door. I stood there like a moron watching him go, then shook myself and helped get Sabrina and Abby awake.

"Come on," I said to Sabrina. "We should get out of here before the police show up."

"The police are the least of your worries, Mr. Black," a familiar voice said from the hallway. The lack of a door was really starting to get on my nerves. I looked up to see the Master of the City standing in the doorway. Greg backed up a lot faster than he'd been walking forward, but at least he didn't run away.

"People have got to quit calling me that. It makes me think my dad has shown up all of a sudden, and that would not be cool." I tried to look a lot less terrified than I actually was. I took a step in front of Sabrina, and Greg motioned for Abby to get behind him.

"I apologize for any respect I may have granted you then, James. Now, what in the world are we to do about you? This makes two consecutive evenings where I have been forced to mesmerize an entire restaurant full of patrons. I simply cannot allow this type of behavior to continue." He stepped into the room and surveyed the damage. "And where shall I send the bill for this cleaning? I understand you are between addresses at the moment."

It wasn't my finest moment. I should have kept my mouth shut in front of the vampire who'd already beaten me to a pulp once that week. But I wasn't known for my discretion. I stepped up to Tiram's face and said, "We would have been done with this last night if you'd bothered to tell us that this douche-rocket was here in your building, instead of making us run all over town looking for him. Then we would only have inconvenienced you for one night, not two."

Tiram looked up at me, eyes wide. He obviously wasn't accustomed to being called out, at least not by anything that wanted to keep living. We stood there, almost nose to chin for the longest few seconds in recent memory, then he did the last thing I expected. He laughed. The Master of the City threw back his head and laughed as if I'd just told the funniest joke since Bill Cosby retired from standup. "Well said, James, well said. You are correct, of course. Had I not been protecting the 'douche-rocket,' as you so eloquently put it, we would not be in this predicament now. But what shall we do about all of this?" He gestured to the mess, including the puddles of dissolving vampire strewn around the apartment.

"Call a cleanup crew and mojo your way out of the bill?" I suggested with a shrug and a lopsided grin.

Tiram cocked his head to the side and laughed again. "Well, of course. But I was referring to them." He pointed more specifically to the vampires we didn't kill. There were a good five or six of them in various states of disrepair, but they'd all heal with enough blood and time out of the sun.

"I don't really care. We didn't kill them, but that's as far ahead as we thought. There were other things we had to take care of, if you know what I mean." I waved a hand at Sabrina, and the Master nodded.

130

"Well, I am short on kitchen help, and they should be able to wash a dish if nothing else. All of you!" He clapped his hands, and the recuperating vamps all stood at attention, or at least managed to stand. "Go downstairs and hide in the walk-in freezer. It has a bolt on the inside of the door, and a five-gallon bucket of blood labeled 'pig testicles' on the top shelf. Try not to spill too much." The survivors made their shuffling way out of the apartment, giving Greg and me wide berth as they did. I didn't blame them. After all, we had kind of shot them just about an hour before.

"So now are we gonna throw down?" I asked Tiram after the last of the walking wounded were out of the way.

"I sincerely hope not. I have come to find you amusing. I'd hate to be forced to destroy you now. Why don't we call a truce, boys? No more killing tonight?" That sounded pretty good to me, so I did what I had learned back in college at Clemson. I spit in my hand and held it out to the Master to shake on it. Tiram looked at my hand as if it were something dead, which it was, but no more dead than *his* hand. So I supposed he looked at it like something dead and stinky. Then he took out his hanky, wiped the spit off my hand, then shook it.

"Okay, then," I said, clasping hands with my new buddy, the Master of the City, in a complicated jive handshake that left him looking at me like a mental deficient. As he tried to disentangle himself, I looked around and said, "What are we all waiting for? Let's go home. Maybe get a little sleep."

"And a shower," Sabrina said, looking disgustedly at her clothes.

"Need help washing your back?" I asked. She glared at me, and I gave her my best innocent smile, which was hampered by the fact that my fangs were still extended. Hey, I was hungry. Really.

"As soon as I do, Jimmy, you'll be the first to know." She smiled a little at me as we all walked down the hall to the elevator.

Chapter 27

It was a little surreal riding in an elevator with the Master of the City. This was the same guy who'd stood by as Krysta tossed my best friend off a roof, the same guy who hid The Professor from us while Sabrina was his captive. Every instinct in my body told me I needed to kill the guy. Well, every instinct except the ones that were screaming to run away from him as fast as my size elevens would carry me. For his part, Tiram just stood in the elevator like anyone else, watching the numbers change and whistling a little tune.

"So, how did you become the Master of the City?" I asked in a feeble attempt at small talk.

"I killed my predecessor," Tiram said simply. Greg shot me a look that said, *Do not piss off the badass super-vamp.*

I didn't take the hint. "Why? Just to run Charlotte? Or did he do something to you?"

"He was the Master. I wanted to be. It was impossible for me to become Master while he yet lived, so I solved the problem. And now, gentlemen, I bid you adieu." He bowed gracefully to Sabrina as the doors slid open behind him. "Detective," he said, making a grand gesture for her to exit the elevator.

That gesture froze in mid-swoop as he caught sight of King and Krysta squaring off in the lobby. In the middle of a giant atrium of marble and glass, the werewolf and my vampire mommy looked like a couple of prizefighters circling, looking for the right moment to strike. Krysta had the lobby guard by the throat, using his body as a shield, and King was circling her trying to get a good shot. He had his AR-15 at his shoulder, and the assault rifle looked like a toy in the hands of the seven-foot werewolf.

"Crap," I said, heading toward King. "Greg, get Emily out of here! Abby, go find us some transportation. It needs to seat at least six. Sabrina, cover me. Tiram—"

"I will do as I will, Mr. Black," the Master Vampire snapped.

"Fine, just don't get in my way. Let me deal with King." I turned to face the Master, and he held up both hands with a slight smile on his face. Out of the corner of one eye, I saw Greg pulling Emily from behind the guard's desk and hustling her out the front doors. Abby was long gone and, with Greg keeping Emily safe, I could concentrate on the big furry problem at hand.

"I wouldn't dream of interfering." He leaned against the wall beside the elevators, arms folded as I headed toward King.

"King, what's going on?" I asked, as I came into his peripheral vision.

"What does it look like, Jimmy? I'm going to kill this bloodsucking bitch." He never took his eyes off Krysta, who kept an equally sharp focus on King. The guard looked at me as if I were Santa Claus, the Tooth Fairy, and Jesus Christ all rolled into one. Yet he was the one I was least likely to save. At least he wasn't likely to have to live with the disappointment.

"I can't let you kill her, King. That's not how we work." I stepped directly into the line of fire and held up both hands so he'd see that I was unarmed. I didn't expect him to believe it, of course, but not holding a weapon at that second was the closest he was going to come to me being unarmed. I had a Glock 17 in the back waistband of my pants and a magical sword hanging off my belt, but I wasn't sure I'd be able to take King if it really came down to it. I knew I didn't have any silver ammo, but I wasn't sure what he'd loaded up with, and I didn't want to think about the damage he could do with the bowie knife on his belt. In my hands, it would be a short sword. In King's, it was more like a toothpick. But the rifle was my first concern, mostly because it was pointed right at my face.

King took a couple of steps forward. I took a couple in the other direction to counter, but heard Krysta whisper from behind me. "Don't get too close, or he'll shoot through you to kill me." I didn't bother telling her that an AR-15 didn't have that kind of punch, because I really had no idea.

"Stop right there, Kyle. I don't want to hurt you. But I'm not going to let you murder her." He lowered the rifle an inch or two and looked at me as if I were nuts. That seemed to be the look I was getting the most this week.

"Putting that monster down won't be murder, Jimmy. It'll be public service." He raised the gun again as he spoke.

I drew my pistol and aimed it at his left knee. "I don't have any ammo that will kill you, Kyle, but I bet putting a round through that kneecap won't be much fun if it's silver or lead. Now lower the weapon."

He lowered it, but asked, "Why are you protecting her? You just shot, slashed, and stomped your way through a bloodbath of biblical proportions, and now you've got a conscience? Is this some kind of vampire unity thing? Am I going to have to kill you, too? Because she dies tonight. Or I do. There's no third option."

"There's always another option, King. What's your beef with Krysta, anyway? I know why I want to kill her, but what did she do to you?" I tried to keep him talking until I could come up with a brilliant plan, but it looked more and more like that was going to take longer than I had. Like a year or two.

"She tried to turn my wife," King replied, and brought the rifle back to bear on Krysta's face.

"What do you mean, tried?" I asked. "It's not really something you can screw up. You drain someone to death; they come back a vampire. That's what happens."

"Not if that someone is a werewolf," King said simply.

"Okay, look, man. I understand that I'm not the sharpest knife in the drawer, but I need a little more explanation than that. Krysta tried to turn your wife, and it didn't work? That should mean that she's still alive, right?"

"We're immune to the magic that makes vampires, Jimmy," King said in a flat, dead voice. I looked up into his yellow eyes and saw the pain there. Tears welled up, and he reached one paw over to dash them away. I snatched away the rifle, bent the barrel, and tossed it across the lobby. King's hand flew to his bowie knife, but I caught his wrist before he drew it.

"No." I said. "We aren't murderers. We're better than that."

"I'm not," he said through clenched teeth. Then he punched me in the gut with his other hand, and I flew a good three feet before I hit the floor. I shook my head to clear the cobwebs then stood up, facing King.

"Ouch. Now let me make this very clear. I have prior claim on Krysta. If anyone kills her, it's going to be me. And it will not be tonight. And if you have a problem with that, then we should deal with it right now." I pulled a pair of knives from my arm sheaths.

"So be it, Jimmy. Hate it had to go this way, but that bitch dies tonight, and anyone in my way dies with her." He drew that massive bowie knife and let out a roar that shook the windows.

We charged.

Everything I knew about knife fights I had learned watching Jackie Chan movies and *Deadliest Warrior* reruns. By the way he swung his giant toothpick at my head, King had a little more practical experience. So I figured I'd have to do what I always did when I was outclassed in a fight—cheat. As the werewolf charged, I did the most counterintuitive thing in the world, I threw away my weapon. Of course, I threw it right at King, so there was a point to it.

Pun totally intended. The knife sank hilt-deep into the werewolf's shoulder, and he paused for about half a step to yank it out and toss it aside. I waited until he was almost on top of me, then jumped straight up into the air, using my height and vamp-strength to my advantage. King slashed at my feet, but I was a dozen feet in the air and climbing by the time he got to me. I twisted around in midair and came down behind the wolfman, who ignored me and kept charging straight for Krysta. Krysta responded just as I expected, by throwing the guard at King and running for the hills. I tossed my other knife at his furry back, and he drew up short as the new blade sunk to the hilt in his muscled flesh. King caught the guard and set him down before turning to deal with me.

"I guess we're going to have to resolve this little disagreement before I move on to the main event," he growled.

"Gotta get through the undercard first, Rocky." I drew my sword and hoped it wouldn't turn King to dust if I cut him with it.

"I don't want to hurt you, Jimmy." I'd always noticed that the people who said things like that were always people who intended to hurt me quite badly.

"And I don't want to get hurt, so why don't we just call this off and grab a beer?" I gestured toward the street outside. "There's a great brewery just a couple blocks from here. You'd have to de-fur, though. I think they have a no pets rule."

King just snarled and charged me again, leaping the last ten feet to block my jump. I just stood there, waiting for him to land, then stepped to the side as soon as he got to me, slashing toward his right hamstring with my sword. He twisted at the last second and caught my blade on his, twisting my sword aside and leaving me open. With his left hand, he landed a shot to my jaw that spun me completely around and made my ears ring. I recovered quickly enough to drop to the ground and slash at his ankles, but he hopped over my attack easily and kicked me in the jaw on the way up.

I flopped onto my back and sprawled on the cold marble floor, dropping my sword in the process. King landed nimbly in front of me and sneered down at me. "Not used to fighting someone who's as fast and strong as you are, vampire?"

"Not used to fighting someone who smells like a wet cocker spaniel, furball." I spat a little blood out along with the wisecrack, then quickly rolled to one side as the big bowie knife slammed into the floor where I'd been lying. I picked up my sword as I rolled over it, came up behind King, and drove the mystical blade through the back of one leg. He howled in pain and swept a huge furred arm across my chest. I flew about eight feet before landing flat on my back again, this time cracking my skull on the floor.

After a couple of seconds, the stars cleared from my vision

enough for me to see King limping toward me, bowie knife in one hand and my sword in the other. I tried to stand, but a wave of dizziness took over, and I went back down on one knee. King got to where I was kneeling and tossed my sword aside to snatch me up by the collar of my jacket. The sudden motion made the room spin again as he held me high over his head and drew back for a finishing blow with his bowie knife. The combination of the spinning room and the pain from my other injuries left me with only one move, so I used it.

Just as King slashed forward to gut me with his pig-sticker, I puked square in his face. A fountain of frozen blood from dinner earlier cascaded into his eyes, nose, and open mouth. The werewolf dropped me straight down onto my face as he tried to wipe the blood from his eyes. I lay there for a second or two listening to the werewolf curse before I got enough equilibrium back to stand up fast, landing an uppercut to King's testicles on the way.

The big wolf collapsed, wiping his face with one paw and holding his crushed groin with the other. As he went down, I put my right kneecap through his nose. His head hit the stone with a sickening crack, and his eyes rolled back in his head. The bowie knife skittered across the lobby. After a couple of seconds, I heard a slow, sarcastic clapping and looked up to see Tiram walking slowly toward me.

"Well done, James. I thought the part where you vomited on your opponent was truly inspired." He offered me a handkerchief. I wiped the blood from my lips and passed it back to him. "Keep it," he said with a small hand gesture.

"Thanks. I came up with that move all on my own. We gonna fight now? 'Cause if so, you win." I put the handkerchief in a back pocket and walked over to where Krysta had been watching the fight. She'd obviously decided that hanging around the superior firepower was a good move, because I found her holed up behind the guard station with Sabrina and all the guns.

"My hero," she gushed, throwing her arms around my neck.

I pushed her away, none too gently. "Lay off. I hooked up with you before. It didn't end well. Why didn't you run?"

"It needed to end, one way or the other. Now that you've beaten him, I'll drain him, and we'll be done with this silliness once and for all." She started toward where King lay helpless, and I caught her arm. She struggled for a minute until Sabrina tapped her on the shoulder with a shotgun and raised one eyebrow meaningfully. Apparently, there had been a conversation while all the fighting was going on.

136

"I said nobody else dies tonight, and I meant it. Now, we're leaving, and you're leaving town. If I ever see you again, or even hear about you turning anyone else in my city, you're dust." I held out a hand for Sabrina, and we started for the door.

"Your city, James?" Tiram asked. "If I didn't know better, I'd think that sounded like a power play on your part."

Chapter 28

I turned and walked over to the Master of the City. "I don't care how it sounds, Tiram. This is the deal. She has until midnight tomorrow night to get the hell out of Charlotte. After that, if I ever see her, smell her, or hear rumor of her anywhere near this town, I'll stake her myself. This is a one-time pass, a limited-time offer. And if you don't like that, we can dance right now." I was bluffing, of course. Tiram could take me on my best day, and my best day would always be one that didn't include a fistfight with a werewolf.

The Master looked at me thoughtfully for a long moment, then surveyed the lobby. King was starting to come around, Sabrina was still packing at least one pistol, and Greg had come back into the building once it was safe for Emily. Krysta shot the Master a look of appeal, but he shrugged and finally said, "As you wish, James. Krysta, my hospitality is hereby revoked. You are forbidden to remain in my city past midnight tomorrow, and you may never return under pain of death." He looked back at me. "Happy?"

"Thrilled," I replied, turning and heading back to the door. I made it about halfway across the lobby before an enraged Krysta got up the nerve to charge me, screaming like a banshee. I braced for another fight but, before I had a chance to slug my maker in the face a few times, she was tackled by a blond streak that moved faster than any vampire I'd ever seen, including Tiram.

Abby drove a shoulder into Krysta's gut and kept right on going, running full speed into an elevator with the elder vampire taking all the force of the impact. Then, she unleashed a savage beating on her vamp-mother. It was no hair-pulling, eye-gouging chick fight; it was vampire claws, fangs, and superhuman speed. Krysta looked like a frog in a blender as Abby rained punch after punch on her face, then commenced to banging her head against the polished marble floor. Less than a minute into the fight, Krysta was out cold, and Abby was up and headed to where King had rolled to one side to watch the carnage.

"Move," she snarled at the werewolf, and he scooted quickly out of her way. She picked up the bowie knife where King had dropped it, and started back to where Krysta lay moaning, both legs broken, and probably her skull as well. I dashed to intercept Abby, but she stiff-armed me into a wall, and I sat down hard, seeing little birds and stars for about the fifth time that night.

Abby stalked over to Krysta, stood over her, and said, "This is where Jimmy would say something annoying, but I don't care enough to come up with a joke." She grabbed the vampiress by the hair with her left hand, pulled her into a sitting position, and cut off her head. She dropped the head a couple of feet away from the body, tossed the knife to land near King, and turned to walk out the front door.

"I have an Escalade. It seats seven. Let's go." She didn't look back at any of us as she headed out the door, and we all just watched her go. After a couple of seconds, Sabrina, Greg, and Emily followed her wordlessly out to the waiting car, leaving me alone in the lobby with the Master of the City and a werewolf that I'd beaten half to death.

I groaned as I got to my feet, then looked over at Tiram. "We're not going to have any problems between us after this, are we?" I gestured to Krysta's rapidly dissolving corpse.

"She was no longer protected by my hospitality. I care nothing for what happened to her."

"And Professor?" I went on. If the guy was going to come after me, I wanted to know about it.

"He and his band of morons had become an annoyance. By destroying them, you performed a service. That service almost balances the cost of the mess you created. Almost. I will not seek redress for the money you have cost me, and you are free to live in Professor's house, but the apartment here reverts to me. And I expect you to stay out of my wine cellar."

"Most days," I promised.

"Fair enough." He pressed a button for the elevator and got in as I turned to face King. The big wolfman had regained his feet and sheathed his bowie knife. He was human again, mostly naked, covered in blood and puke. He stood over Krysta's body, watching her turn to dust and slowly stroking the gold band on his left ring finger.

"We good?" I asked.

"Yeah, we're good."

"Thanks for your help tonight."

"Don't sweat it."

"Sorry I kicked your ass."

"Don't sweat that either." We stood there for a long minute before the last bits of Krysta disappeared into a pile on the stone floor.

"What's next for you?" I asked.

"Go home. See about putting my life back together. Stay the hell away from vampires." He held out a hand. I looked at it for a second, then gave it a shake.

"You're not bad for a soulless bloodsucking fiend, Black," he said, as we walked out the front door. He turned left to where his truck was parked at an expired meter, tore up the tickets under his windshield wiper, and got in. He fired up the truck and pulled a U-turn in the middle of the busy street, peeling rubber as he headed off to start over.

"You're not bad, either, King. For an overgrown Peekapoo," I murmured as I got into the passenger seat of the Escalade.

We'd gone about a mile before my curiosity overwhelmed me and I looked over at Abby. "Where'd the car come from?"

"It's on loan from the bank. Or I guess it's on loan from a banker. He let me borrow it for a week while he's on vacation." She giggled a little.

"Where did he go?" I asked, my head full of visions of dead bankers littering downtown.

"Nowhere. But he's going to think he went to Aruba and let me borrow his car. Don't worry, Jimmy, I didn't kill him. Just mojoed him a little." She reached over and patted my leg. "I know how testy you get about killing the entrees."

"I get testy about killing everyone, Abby. So you want to explain why you beat Krysta into paste?" I looked over at her, and her face had gone grave and very still. It looked as though she was getting the hang of being a vampire. I wasn't sure I liked that.

"She killed me. I killed her back. Sounds fair to me," she said, not looking at me. I stared at her for another mile or two, and she finally cracked. I'd had more time to practice the stony vampire stare, and she wilted under my impassive gaze. "Please don't hate me, Jimmy," she whispered, a pale pink tear rolling down her cheek. "I lost it. I saw her coming at you, and I just lost it. I couldn't stand the thought of her hurting you, and then I couldn't stand the thought of her hurting anyone else. I had her down, she was beaten, but she looked up at me at the end and smirked at me, as though nothing I did mattered. That's what did it. I had to wipe that smirk off her stupid face." Abby pulled the SUV into a parking space near our new house and sat there, head on the steering wheel, shoulders shaking.

I reached over and clumsily patted her on the shoulder for a second or two. She glanced up at me, smiling like she'd just won the lottery or something. "Gotcha!" Abby yelled, peals of laughter filling the cab of the Escalade. "Seriously, Jimmy, did you really buy all that navel-gazing crap? I was *pissed*. Sure, I didn't want her hurting you, but the bottom line is, that bitch killed me, so I returned the favor.

Now let's go have a beer. We won this one!" She got out of the truck and slammed the door behind her. I looked back at Sabrina and saw the furrowed brow and worried look on her face that mirrored my own.

"We'll take care of this later," I said, opening my own door. "For now, a beer sounds really good."

Chapter 29

I sat on the steps of the frat house, cold beer in my hand and Sabrina by my side, as we stared at the stolen Escalade across the parking lot. Greg and his sister sat on the tailgate for a long time before they got up. He hugged her for a long moment, then I saw him stare into her eyes and walk back to the frat house. Emily walked across the lot, got into a new-ish Prius and drove off without seeming to notice we were there.

"You all right?" I asked Greg, as I handed him a beer.

"Nope." He twisted off the cap and flicked it into the distance.

"You want to talk about it?" Sabrina asked, leaning around me to stare at my partner. Her brown hair fell in front of her furrowed brow, and I absently reached over to tuck it behind her ear. She caught my hand as I brought it back down and held it while she watched for Greg's response.

"Nope." He drained his beer and reached for another. I passed him one from the cooler behind Sabrina and watched as he sucked it down, too. It wasn't as though he could get drunk off a few beers, or even a whole lot of beers, but drinking as an Olympic event was more my speed than Greg's.

We sat there in silence looking up at the stars for a long time. Okay, we were doing more airplane-watching than star-gazing, since we were still in the city, but it was still pretty nice to sit still after the week we'd had. I was enjoying the quiet and the warmth of Sabrina's hand in mine when Greg spoke again.

"I mojo'd her," he murmured.

"You had to," I said.

"I know, but it sucks."

"Yeah, but it sucks less than her waking up tomorrow and knowing the truth. That doesn't do anybody any good." I put a hand on his shoulder, but he shrugged me off.

"I hate this, you know? This whole thing. I hate it. I know you think it's cool, being a detective, playing superhero. But it's not. There's nothing cool about this. There's just doing what we can to make it suck as little as possible, and maybe help somebody else out along the way. That's all we've got. We don't get to grow up. We don't get to have families. We just get to play video games and run around in stolen cars and watch our friends die. And I hate it. And I hate you for doing this to me." Greg never looked at me. He just stared straight ahead and let the heat in his voice carry through the whispered words.

I stared at him, not knowing what to say. After a minute that stretched into hours, all I came up with was a whispered, "I'm sorry."

"I know," he said. "And most days, that's enough. Most days, I can deal with being twenty-two and fat forever, with never being able to meet a girl who might actually like me, with never going to the beach with my kids someday like my parents did with me. Most days, I'm okay with it. But today's not that day. Today, I want to meet my little sister's fiancé. Today, I want to see her graduate in May. Today, I want to be the big brother that looks out for her all the time, not just at night. Today... I want to kill your sorry ass." He stood up and went into the house. A few seconds later, I heard a door slam in the basement and knew that he had locked himself in a room.

"He'll be okay," Sabrina said.

"Yeah."

"He didn't mean that."

"Yeah, he did. And he's right. I did this to him. I lost control and killed my best friend, and now he's got to put up with my mistake forever."

"You didn't know. You couldn't know."

"Doesn't matter, does it? It's done. I took everything away from him. He didn't deserve that. Nobody does."

"Life sucks, wear a helmet," Sabrina replied in a steely voice.

I whipped my head around to stare at her, openmouthed. After a second of doing my best fish out of water impression, I asked, "What?"

"Life's hard, Jimmy. You can wallow in it, or you can move on. No, it's not fair that you got turned into a vampire right out of college. It's not fair that you went nuts and drained your best friend, and now you guys are stuck in a bizzarro *Friends* episode forever. It's not fair that Mike has cancer, or that Abby got turned before she graduated, or that my gay cousin is really a changeling from FairyLand, or that my boyfriend is an undead monster. But this is the hand we were dealt. You made a choice. You chose to help people. You could have decided to be a psycho like Krysta, or a coldblooded ass like Tiram, but you decided to take all your crap and do some good with it. So quit whining and play the game." She reached into the cooler, got two more beers, and handed one to me. I sat there staring at her for another minute, then twisted the top off my beer and took a long swallow.

"Thanks," I said, after a good healthy belch.

"No problem. Reality checks are my specialty."

"Now, about that boyfriend comment?" I asked, eyebrows reaching for my hairline.

"Shut up and kiss me, you idiot."

So I did.

For a long time.

.

Acknowledgements

As always, this book would not have been possible without the love and support of my amazing wife, Suzy. There are a few other folks I'd like to take a moment to mention here. First off, my fantastic editor Lynn O'Dell of Red Adept Reviews, who made this book tighter, cleaner and (hopefully) typo-free. The work that she and her merry band of proofreaders performed for me was nothing short of incredible, and I look forward to using them again.

I've got to give a big shout out to my buddy Curtis Krumel for suggesting the name of the book. It's fairly obvious that I'm working on a theme here, and Curtis gave me this title.

Thanks to Valerie Huffman for the initial beta-read, I appreciate her help in letting me know if I was too far off track with the book. And thanks to everyone who has read the first few books and become friends with Jimmy, Greg, Sabrina and Mike. I love these characters, and it makes a poor author feel fantastic to know that you guys do too.

As always, you can find me online at www.johnhartness.com, and you can email me at johnhartness@gmail.com.

Thanks!

John G. Hartness
August 5, 2011

Made in the USA
Charleston, SC
17 May 2012